P9-DJK-355

THE
Taker's Stone

/ / /

A MELANIE KROUPA BOOK

WITHDRAWN
LVC BISHOP LIBRARY

THE
Taker's Stone

/ / /

BARBARA TIMBERLAKE RUSSELL

A DK INK BOOK
DK PUBLISHING, INC.

A *Melanie Kroupa* Book

DK Publishing, Inc.
95 Madison Avenue
New York, New York 10016

Visit us on the World Wide Web at http://www.dk.com

Copyright © 1999 by Barbara Timberlake Russell

All rights reserved. No part of this publication may be reproduced or
transmitted in any form or by any means, electronic, photocopying,
recording, or otherwise, without the prior written permission
of the publisher.

Library of Congress Cataloging-in-Publication Data
Russell, Barbara T.
  The taker's stone / by Barbara Timberlake Russell. — 1st ed.
    p.   cm.
  Summary: When fourteen-year-old Fischer accidentally uses a magic
stone to summon Thistle, one of its Keepers and an agent of the Light,
he must help her fight the evil Belial, who seeks to rule the world with
cruel darkness.
  ISBN 0-7894-2568-8
  [1. Fantasy.]   I. Title.
PZ7.R91536Tak 1999   98-24022
[Fic]—dc21   CIP
                                                          AC

Book design by Chris Hammill Paul.
The text of this book is set in 13 point Centaur.
Printed and bound in U.S.A.

First Edition, 1999
2 4 6 8 10 9 7 5 3 1

To Betsy, Lynn, and Nancy

One wall makes a shield, four walls a fortress–B. T. R.

/ / /

ANNUS MIRABILIS, "YEAR OF WONDERS"

/ / /

A term often associated with the phenomena of 1811, when a profusion of tornadoes and the onset of "ungodly heat" were chronicled. A double-tailed comet was seen over France, entire forests fell, and a mass migration of squirrels was sighted in Kentucky. In addition, the world was plagued with earthquakes, such as the New Madrid, Missouri, earthquake, which caused the Mississippi River's flow to change direction. No one really knows why these phenomena occurred, but a 1983 *Time* magazine article explained it most succinctly: "The prevailing opinion, for a little while, was that the universe had gone crazy."

Be sober, be vigilant; because your adversary the devil, as a roaring lion, walketh about, seeking whom he may devour. —*1 Peter 5:8*

France
1811

PROLOGUE

Out of a darkness marred only by countless stars came the sound of distant flapping. If it had been earlier in the day, the laborers who picked the grapes in this valley might have speculated that it was only the beginnings of the mistral across the mountains or falcons slowing their flight to land in hidden nests in the rocks. But at this hour of night there were no men or women in the vineyards, no monks awake in the monastery to observe the disturbance.

Within moments a roll of thunder sent a flurry of rubble tumbling down the sides of the immense mountain peak. Clouds gathered over the summit, crowning it, and somewhere in their middle, a dark tunnel opened to the sky. Now the flapping was accompanied by the smell of myrrh and lavender and funeral oils. Suddenly a figure materialized from within the clouds and stepped onto the snow.

Covered only by a dark swath of cloth across its hips, it

was neither man nor woman. The features of its face were vaguely formed. Wings, darkly veined as a dragonfly's, extended from a place below ashen shoulders. Lightning flashed, and the figure opened its arms.

It metamorphosed first into a short, elderly man with sagging skin, then an ample-hipped woman with long red hair, then a child—a boy with brilliant turquoise eyes—then a pigtailed girl holding a hoop that became in turn a porcelain doll, a jumping rope, a ball. After a moment of this fluctuation, the wind settled, the clouds drew back, and the wings on the creature withdrew with a sound like crumpling paper. The remaining figure, a man, opened his eyes. They were covered with a cloudy film, and the skin on his face was smeared with bits of blood and the milky curd found on newborns.

Overhead only wisps remained of the clouds. The film on the man's eyes evaporated. He blinked, then reached into his pocket and found a cloth that he used to wipe clean his face and manicured beard. His fingers ran through his hair, as fine and dark as that of the rodents he had recently eaten.

A moment later, as though he were a weather vane, his feet pivoted, making a grinding noise in the grit. He raised his nose into the wind, and his dark eyes focused above. In the sky a twin-tailed comet scarred the night.

He could not smell her, but she was there, Thistle, truly her mother's whelp. She was alone, now, secreted away, but he would find her. He longed to silence her for eternity, as he had her mother. His soldiers sought Solomon now. It wouldn't be long until his old enemy was reduced to nothing more than dust.

The light in the sky flared, revealing a vision. A face—all flame—a boy with outstretched hand, but holding what? The image was distorted, defying the focus of his mind's eye as a moth fluttering under the shadow of a fingertip. The man growled and circled in agitation. He sensed the pull of the Stones, his driving force, even then. With only one Keeper remaining, he was closer than he had ever been to possessing the Stones. He smelled opportunity, then danger, but could not discern which was the greater. The man threw back his head, and a thunderous howl shattered the silence. A moment later the vision disappeared, and again a double-tailed comet shone in the northern sky, leaving nothing to read but stars in the perfect darkness.

/ / /

Welcome back from another set of continuous, mar-velous music. We've got you hooked in to WBST, the best of the South, and I've got to tell you, that is one gor-G-ous night we've got going out there, people. So, if you're putting together some weekend plans—a little waterski-ing, the outdoor concert at the amphitheater, or maybe you're just planning on taking that somebody special on a moonlit walk—well, you can count yourself among the blessed. Clear skies tonight, a balmy seventy-five de-grees, hotter during the day tomorrow, but with those same blue skies in our five-day extended forecast. So get out there and enjoy, people. It doesn't get much better than this.

/ / /

*For wisdom is better than jewels, and
all that you may desire cannot compare
with her.   —Proverbs 8:11*

CHAPTER ONE

In his dreams the man was always cloaked in shadow. And
sometimes, like tonight, Fischer awoke with the sensation
of a searing pain that emerged from somewhere deep inside him. He shoved down his covers and scrambled to the
window, but no one was there, no one.

Through the filigree of branches across the back lawn,
the moon was rising. Fischer turned off his Walkman and
picked up the book he had fallen asleep reading, *Primitive
Civilizations.* It was the book his father had sent, his latest
guilt offering for not being home that summer. He found
his place on the page, but it was no use. Like his cousin
David's beloved computer, his mind downloaded all his
worries, so that during these sleepless hours they could
scroll over and over in his head. Lately this list consisted of
his very pregnant mother; his father, absent as usual; and,
last but not least, David.

Fischer perched on the wooden desk that overlooked the

line of front yards on the quiet street below. Maybe he and David had spent too many summers together. Since Grandpa had died, Fischer didn't want to spend time with anyone, and especially not with David for a monthlong summer vacation. He was happy just helping his mother set up the displays at the museum.

"You won't have much fun staying home with me, kiddo," his mother had said, patting his hand and then her stomach. "I've delayed the Incas exhibit till August. Go to White Horse. Then, when it's time for the baby, Aunt Kathy and Uncle Matt will drive you and David back to Leeland. You won't miss a thing."

Fischer finally agreed. It seemed to make his mother feel better to think that he would be having a good time in White Horse instead of being "stuck" at home. Then suddenly it was July, and Fischer had no choice but to go.

The door to Fischer's room creaked open.

"Ready?" David whispered. His dark hair fell over his face as he stepped inside and closed the door behind him. "Hey, you're not even dressed."

"That's because I was hoping you would forget," Fischer said.

"Not a chance." While Fischer pulled on his T-shirt, David flipped open Fischer's Walkman and examined the CD. "Fischer," he said, "what have I told you? The blues are for the terminally sad and catatonic." He slapped the lid down again and threw Fischer a pair of jeans. "Lighten up, all right?" A smile spread across David's face; it was the one that had always prompted ice cream from relatives, quarters from strangers, and now that he was almost fifteen, an assortment of girls' hearts. "I hope you don't act this way when we're with James on Saturday."

More fun, Fischer thought as he remembered the camping trip Aunt Kathy had arranged for their "last summer blast." This time he would have to endure not only David but his friend, a loud, swaggering kid appropriately named James Black.

"Teenagers are supposed to do things for no apparent reason," David said. "If we didn't, our parents would be out of a job. Come on, Fischer, tonight is going to be great, I swear."

"Right. Great." Fischer had planned to tell David that he had no intention of sneaking out tonight, but when he looked David in the eye, he couldn't. Why did he always feel as if he were the older of the two, instead of the other way around? "But what if something goes wrong?"

"Like what?" David studied him with a look that moved beyond disappointment and inched toward contempt. "Are you sure we're part of the same family? You don't like to do anything."

I like plenty, Fischer thought, recalling how bored David had looked when he had shown him around the museum last summer. Just not what you like to do.

He thought of arguing this point but instead turned to

pull on his jeans and saw his own muted reflection in the window glass next to his cousin's. Straight hair, wide eyes—largely forgettable. He had shot up over the summer but added only a few pounds to his frame.

"Listen, while you're here, out of your pathetic norm, be a little daring for once. Come on." David motioned to Fischer, then held open the door. "It'll be like old times."

For a moment Fischer remembered how much he had once looked forward to summers with David, back when they were little, playing cops and robbers in the backyard. So maybe it was for the sake of old times that Fischer grabbed his blue jeans jacket and followed David out the door, down the dim stairway, through the kitchen, still fragrant with rosemary from Aunt Kathy's chicken dinner, and down another creaking set to the cool basement of the house.

Fischer's stomach tightened at the sight of the moon through the mud-splattered window. It illuminated a chipped utility tub and a tilted washing machine flanking the narrow wall. Between them, in the draft created from gaps in a glass-slatted door, spiderwebs wafted. Why am I doing this? Fischer wondered.

David inserted a key into the dead bolt, turned it with some effort, and scraped the door open over the dirt of the cracking linoleum floor.

Finding a broom in a corner of the room, Fischer batted down a web, then darted over the threshold. Outside he raced across the yard and pushed through the privet hedge. The empty lot behind the house was gnarled with blackberry brambles that scratched and pulled at him as he ducked into the dense woods. Hearing David's footsteps ahead, he ran faster. Suddenly his foot plunged into something cold and liquid. He shook free from the muddy creek bottom and moved on, this time with his sneaker sole gurgling as it struck the ground. It was what he deserved, allowing David to persuade him to do something he knew he shouldn't. But hadn't he known that and come anyway?

After all, he was older now—fourteen—had a mind of his own, or so his mother told him when she asked his opinion on museum exhibits. Maybe he wasn't the same kind of kid his father, the decorated colonel, had been—or hoped for. Fischer's earliest memories of his father were a series of comings and goings at the airport, with Fischer and his mother waving him off on his next diplomatic assignment, the most recent, two years in the Middle East.

He had duties, responsibilities that kept him away. His father often said that in his letters, but in the last few years Fischer had begun to wonder why he didn't feel any duty or responsibility to Fischer or his mother back home.

All at once there was an opening in the brush, and Fischer saw David, his hands on his hips, a dark cookie-cutter shape at the edge of the trees. The moon behind him was gigantic, round, and tarnished as a coin.

"We're almost there," David called. "Stay low now, and keep up."

Fischer had only a fraction of a second to be annoyed at David for issuing orders before he plunged after him. This time they stooped as they ran, as if they were making for a foxhole on the front lines of a skirmish and not for a band of Gypsies or hoboes or whatever David had heard were camped near the railroad tracks across the field.

They had to slow from running to something akin to wading when the meadow changed from clumps of weed to waist-high grass. Fortunately a breeze blew through a stand of scrawny pines, making a whistling sound that covered the noise of their movements.

Suddenly David held up his hand, and Fischer stopped. His heart pounded dully as he heard voices and saw a distant campfire.

They crawled closer till the crackle of a fire halted them. Now Fischer saw there were really two campfires. The one closer to them was just what he had imagined, a stone-lined blaze encircled by a handful of men in dirty clothes. Behind them, women lay asleep on sheets of cardboard, their children sprawled under their limp arms.

The men spoke together in low voices, a rare laugh erupting, but mostly they stared into the fire, apparently concerned only with stretching their legs or with the to-bacco they tapped into their cigarette papers.

The man nearest to Fischer was dressed in baggy clothes and running shoes. He turned, and his eyes slid over to the bushes where Fischer and David were hiding. Had he seen them? Fischer felt a stab of remorse for being there, for spying on these people, who were here only because of hard times and a lack of money. But a moment later the man turned his back to them again, and Fischer let out his breath. He was headed back to the house. He wasn't going along with David's latest crazy scheme no matter what David would have to say about it.

"Let's go," he whispered. "Now!"

"Hold on, will you?" David ducked away from the cover of brush and motioned Fischer toward the smaller camp-fire, a short distance away. Fischer hesitated. But after a moment of thinking how hard it would be to find his way in the dark, he crouched, moved through the tangle of grass and shrub, and dropped at last next to David behind a tree trunk.

"This is stupid," Fischer said. "Let's go."

David glared. "Give it a minute. We've come this far."

The shorter of the two figures at the campfire, a boy, rose to his feet. He drew a bag from his pocket, tipped it into his hand, and tossed something onto the dying fire.

All at once Fischer felt a roar of heat and fell backward,

righting himself in time to see flames leaping high above the boy's brimmed hat. The orange glow burned an outline of his cloaked figure into the darkness.

"Well, what do you see?" the man asked. As he raised his face to inquire, Fischer saw he was darker-skinned, with a thick mouth and almond-shaped eyes.

"I see the bell," the boy said, his voice oddly high.

The man nodded. "The herald of news."

"No." The boy squatted. "The bell is upside down. And see? In the center flame? The dragon burns beside it."

"Speak then." The man, dressed in a long plain robe, stood up. "Surely you have seen the two as one before."

"Never. But I know their meaning." Fischer and David drew themselves in tight behind the tree as the boy cast a searching look around the brush. "I fear trouble is come."

The man unrolled a blanket and flapped it over the ground. "It is an ill flame. But recall, I built the fire of the things of men: an aged crate and a broken chair. We only feel the trouble of those things; they disturb the flame with their sorrow. It is not a true sign."

The boy shrugged. "Maybe."

"Let us sleep. Tomorrow brings a long journey." The dark man stretched out across his blanket. "I, for one, shall not seek worry. No, if it warrants, worry will seek me well before my rest is done. This I know for truth."

The boy laughed, a musical sound, and emptied a pan

of liquid onto the raging fire. "Well then, I, too, shall rest," he said. The flames extinguished from steam to ash with a single hiss. "But for my own satisfaction, will you check the Stones?"

The man laid a hand on his belly. "They are here, safe." He pulled a pouch from his waistband, shook the contents into his hand, and extended his palm.

Fischer leaned around David to steal a closer look. In the man's hand was an assortment of red stones so luminous that they seemed to radiate into the darkness around them.

"That will do," the boy said. "Put them away. Earlier I heard voices. Perhaps accompanied by curious eyes."

The man began to sift the Stones back into the pouch.

"Do you feel a presence?" the boy asked.

The man turned suddenly toward the first campfire over the hill. "You hear the voices of the vagrants at their own fire." He pulled off his sandals and threw them aside. "The fire has unsettled you. Let us rest. I am old and too weary to do otherwise."

In another moment the boy lowered himself to the grass. He flinched once or twice as though he had heard a sound, but soon he gathered his coat around him and rolled onto his belly, tilting his hat to reveal a hank of pale hair tied with a leather strip. Several moments passed before Fischer heard the baritone snores of the man.

"Did you see that?" David asked. "Looked like gems the

way they glowed, real ones. They've probably pulled a bank heist or robbed somebody's house or something."

"So let's get out of here," Fischer said. "Before they realize we've seen them."

"Are you crazy? I'm not leaving till we get a closer look."

"No, David. Not this time," Fischer said.

David crept out from behind the tree. "Did he put the jewels back in his bag?"

"Forget that. Let's get back before your mom and dad find out we're gone."

The sparkle in David's eyes faded like the fire. "All you've talked about since we left the house is going back."

"That's not true." But Fischer's heart told him otherwise.

"Some great adventurer you turned out to be."

Fischer said nothing. He knew David was referring to the game he and Fischer had played as kids. Each would take a turn planning some feat, plundering hidden gold or rescuing a city from an evil maniac—something courageous that would have to be accomplished for the sake of all mankind. But this was different. This was no game, those stones were no buried treasure, and the guy lying on the blanket was real.

"I'm not afraid, if that's what you're getting at," Fischer said.

David looked skyward, clearly unconvinced.

"I'm not."

"Tell you what, sport," David said. "Why don't you go take a good, close look if you're so brave?"

"No way," Fischer said. But he felt as though his insides had frozen. "I'm not going over there."

"That's what I thought. Everything with you requires a mental rehearsal." David ducked into the grass. "I've had enough of your whining. Let's go."

Fischer started to follow, but then something made him hesitate. His heart pounded at the thought of being left alone, but he knew if he retreated now, he'd never hear the end of it. Adrenaline poured into Fischer's arms and legs as he thought of the look on David's face when he turned back and saw him with the stones in his hand. Then he pictured his own father's face as David told him the story. His father would turn to him with a smile that was both disapproving and approving. "You did that, Fischer? I can hardly believe it." But could Fischer crawl over and look at the stones when everything inside him was telling him to run?

He thought of the times his mother had taken him to the museum at night. While she worked, Fischer plugged Stevie Ray Vaughn into the museum's public-address system and wandered through the exhibits. The Paleolithic Room, the Bronze Age displays, the Neanderthal fossils.

Maybe to someone else, the spotlit shelves of fractured skulls, clay masks, and figurines would be spooky. But Fischer felt at home here, happier really. No one expected anything from him, certainly not conversation, which had never come easy for him with kids his own age. From time to time he would stop and stand completely still. Then he could almost sense a quickening inside him, as though all the fragments of the past released their potency at night, leaving him to absorb them like a sponge. Like the figures in his dreams—the Shadowy Figure and more recently the pale-haired, faceless girl dressed in blue—their secrets buzzed inside his every cell.

If he could summon that power now, maybe he could do it. He could prove to David, and to his father, that he had courage in a way that would earn their admiration once and for all. Before he could change his mind, Fischer crawled out from behind the tree and onto the rough grass surrounding the fire ring.

When he reached the man's blanket, Fischer let his fingers tremble forward. There it was, the pouch, tied to the man's waistband, but lying on the ground beside him. Fischer could hardly believe it. The boy and the man had made such a big deal about hiding the Stones. Was it a trap? If it was, it was too late. He was already prisoner; for some strange reason he felt he *had* to see the Stones. He held the pouch upright, careful not to cause tension between its drawstring and the man's robe, and shook some of the Stones onto the blanket.

Oh, beautiful, beautiful, he thought as he stretched his hand over them. Too beautiful not to touch.

He picked up the first Stone. It glowed warm in his palm. He reached down and picked up another and another, till he had a handful of Stones that tingled his skin with their heat.

Fischer's body felt electrified as the man rolled on his side toward him. Still, he couldn't leave. With the Stones in his hand, he felt in complete control. The moon broke through the cover of a wispy cloud, and now he could make out some of the words scratched onto the pouch.

As Moon and Sun to Earth, so shall the pair hold all
creatures in its balance.
Solomon-Rosemary
Solomon-Thistle

The final name was scratched in a childlike hand so faint Fischer had to squint hard to read it.

He stared down at the Stones. As he held them, a new energy pumped through him. It was as though he were alone in those rooms at the museum again. He had never wanted anything so much. Why couldn't he keep a few for himself?

Suddenly he heard the boy stir and mutter, "Solomon?"

Some of the Stones fell from Fischer's hand and dropped onto the blanket. He stuffed the rest into his pocket and backed away from the fire as the wind in the branches above him made a sound like the intake of breath.

The boy sat up, breathing raggedly. He turned as Fischer stepped into the brush. Then suddenly David's hand clamped down on Fischer's shoulder, and his voice whispered in his ear, "Run!"

When I became a man, I gave up childish ways. For now we see in a mirror dimly, but then face to face.

—1 Corinthians 13:11–12

CHAPTER TWO

Fischer ran, his footfall a counterpoint rhythm to David's. The safety of the forest waited in the distance. His breath pulled in and out, the meadow air becoming a sharp, sweet ache as it filled his lungs. Suddenly he heard a third pattern of steps.

Glancing over his shoulder, Fischer spotted the figure of a man in pursuit. The stars bobbed crazily as Fischer pushed himself faster. Air seemed to swirl with motion around his arms and legs. Could he make it to the silhouette of trees? He had to. Only a hundred feet to go.

"Green thirty-four!" David's voice rose from the night.

For a moment it didn't register. Then Fischer remembered. Green 34. One of Uncle Matt's football plays they'd practiced on the front lawn just this week.

Fischer maneuvered a hairpin turn, hunkered down, waited. When the clouds covered the moon's face, he ran forward, then cut right. Suddenly David was there, barreling full steam for the stranger's middle. The man's face became a mask of exclamation, his eyes suddenly as red as the ones in flash photographs. Fischer shouted his own surprise, then bolted away as the stranger dodged aside, fumbled, and fell.

Inside the cover of branches the denseness of the woods was welcome. Fischer stopped to catch his breath. His head was spinning, and spots danced before his eyes. No wonder he was seeing things.

Out in the field the man scrambled to his feet, slapping his pants leg with his hat. Fischer saw now that it was the man in running shoes from the first campfire. He strained to see how many of the others were in pursuit, but none appeared. His pulse thudded dully inside his neck. Was the man chasing them only because they'd spied on his group?

Then the guy was coming his way again, headed for the woods. Fischer scrambled behind a stump half buried in a muddy bracken, a place where moonlight scarcely found its way through branches to the floor of the wood. The sound of a trickling stream nearby was interrupted by the snap of breaking twigs. A moment later the man's shoes stopped beside the stump. Fischer saw the man tilt his head, then turn in his direction. A shard of moonlight fell onto the man's palm. Fischer spotted a scar, small and round as a quarter.

"You're here now, ain't you, boy?" the man asked.

Fischer did not dare breathe or look up.

"Let's not make a ruckus. You have something, don't you? Ain't yours, ain't mine. It's his. Come out and give it to me, now. I'll deliver it, no harm done. He might even give you and your friend something for your trouble. You'd like that, wouldn't you?"

Fischer stayed frozen in place.

"If you don't come out nice, a nasty bit could come of this. He'll find you. You think I'm the only one who'll be looking for you now? He has a whole army to take care of trouble like you."

Suddenly a voice from the edge of the woods called out, "Joe, is that you? Answer me if you hear me."

"I'm here, Vern," the man beside Fischer called, his voice suddenly brighter. "I thought I saw a light. Somebody snoopin'."

The other man looked over his shoulder. "You ain't lying. Cops are about."

"Coming," the man in running shoes shouted. He took a quick look around, then said in a quieter voice that Fischer knew only he was meant to hear, "But I won't be far, young feller. He'll come when he learns of this." Fischer saw a worried look appear on the man's face. "He can have a temper about matters such as these. Come out, boy. Take my word on this: You'd rather deal with me."

"Joe, come on!"

When Fischer looked up, he saw the man's eyes were only the dark hollows he had seen earlier. He heard the man curse, then saw him duck out of the woods and run across the field toward the campfire with the man called Vern.

Fischer leaned against the tree trunk. He'd almost been found. But he felt strangely exhilarated. For once David couldn't say he hadn't been up for adventure. He laid a hand on the pocket where he'd stuffed the Stones and patted it, then scrambled toward the house.

A short distance ahead he saw the limbs that framed the empty lot behind David's. Home free. Fischer sprinted along the pad of pine needles until his foot hit something hard, a tree root. He fell, then leaped up a moment later with an ache in his knee where he had hit the ground hard.

The Stones! He groped around in the dark. A red glow grew as his hand found the surface of one and then another. He brushed his hand over the ground in search of any others until he heard a branch snap somewhere within the woods. He crammed the Stones back into the side pocket of his jeans jacket, running into the clearing, past the wall of privet hedge, and through the familiar backyard to the laundry room door.

As Fischer stumbled in, David shoved the door closed and locked it, rattling the louvered glass. David raised a hand. "Shhhh."

The sound was issued like another of David's orders,

but despite his irritation, Fischer waited for the same thing David did: the sound of footsteps creaking the wood planks of the upstairs hallway. After a moment of silence David let out a long sigh, and Fischer slumped to the floor in a heap.

"You ditch him?"

"Barely," Fischer said. "That was close."

"That's an understatement. How could you be that stupid?"

Fischer stared, dumbstruck by David's disapproval.

"Back there at the fire, Fish Head." It was the nickname Fischer despised. "You could have gotten us killed."

Fischer put his hand in his pocket and felt the smooth surface of two Stones. David was jealous. But that figured. He was always the one in the spotlight, the daredevil, the intrepid hero. Now that the shoe was on the other foot and it was Fischer's moment, David *would* insist on trying to make Fischer feel like an idiot.

He pulled himself upright, his cheeks flaming hot with anger. "You're the one who wanted me to get a 'good, close look.'"

"Well, I didn't think you would *take* them," David said.

The surface of the washer felt cool against Fischer's back. Why let David spoil his moment of triumph? "Well, I did. And I've got them here. They're mine." He patted his pocket. "But you can have a look." He pulled out the

Stones, and as he admired their fiery red color, something inside him seemed to bend toward them.

"So that's how the little guy did the flame trick. Here, let me see them."

Fischer folded his fingers over the Stones. "These aren't trick Stones." It was the same reaction he had when people called the bronze and silver figurines at the museum trinkets.

David frowned. "How do you know?" He stood and rooted around on the utility shelf till he found a pack of matches, an old can, and some stacks of newspaper. Setting the can in the middle of the floor between him and Fischer, David lit the paper in the coffee can and blew lightly till a fire crackled. He looked Fischer squarely in the eye. "Well?" David held out his hand. "Give, genius. I'll throw it in."

Fischer felt confident with the Stones clasped in his palm, stronger than he could ever remember. He knew the Stones' worth; he could feel it. He opened his hand to look at them one more time. Suddenly David reached over, snatched a Stone, and tossed it into the flame.

The fire scattered, producing nothing more than a puff of sparks. Fischer smothered the flames with an old dustpan and poked a stick into the charred paper. What if he'd lost the Stone for good? Despite the lingering heat, he plunged his hand into the coffee can, found the warmth of a smooth surface, and lifted it out. The Stone was still perfect. Better yet, now it was his again. Something inside his chest relaxed as he rubbed the Stone against his shirt and held it high to admire its shine.

"I told you." Fischer smiled, trying to cover his momentary panic. "They're not trick."

David raised an eyebrow. "Well, they must be good for something."

"Maybe not." Behind his back Fischer rolled the Stones inside his hand. What could he say to divert David's interest away from them? "Maybe they're just great fakes."

David looked skeptical. "Think, Fischer. If they were fakes, would those two weirdos back at the fire be so worried about them?"

Fischer shrugged. His mind filled with possibilities to explore later when he had the Stones in his room, alone, and David was asleep. "They might be gems, like you said. We could take them in town tomorrow and ask at the jewelry shop."

"Stones that glow? Haven't seen any of those around town, have you?" David sprawled on his side. "They're like the things we used to read about in fairy tales. You know? Magic things."

Fischer remembered an Egyptian piece that had come into the museum last year. Supposedly it had a long history of bringing its owner good luck, but he'd never believed it.

"Remember Aladdin? He got three wishes from the

lamp. I know this is over the edge, Fish Head, but maybe—" He sat up and looked hard at Fischer. "Maybe we could get stuff from those Stones."

"Wishing Stones?" Fischer made a face and squeezed his fist around the Stones until he thought he might draw blood. He suddenly felt as though he couldn't let the Stones go even if he wanted to, and he didn't want to, least of all for David.

"Look, we've got nothing to lose. Nobody except you and me is ever going to know what happened tonight. Or is something else stopping you?" David observed Fischer through narrowed eyelids. "Like maybe you're scared of what could happen?"

Fischer looked up and saw what he knew he would see, David's taunting smile, the same smile that had dared Fischer to stick his hand into a dark hole in a tree stump when he was seven and to ride his bike through the cemetery after dark when he was ten. Fischer felt anger seep through him. Suddenly he didn't feel any older than the first time he had come to stay in White Horse. He was still stuck between doing something he desperately didn't want to do and proving himself to David.

"I'm still waiting," David said. "Fish Head. Or is it . . . Chicken Little?"

Fischer felt the bars close around him. He pushed away his objections, his fingers trembling as they released a Stone into David's hand.

"That's better." David shook the red Stone in his hand like a die over a game board. "Oh, mighty potentate, I want—"

"Just do it," Fischer commanded.

"Money!" David beamed at his own brilliance. "I wish for money, greenback, coin, whatever you want to call it." He threw the Stone into the fire. Again, nothing more appeared than smoke and a dusting of ash. "Now you."

For an instant Fischer tried to forget the way the Stones made him feel and concentrated on what his wish would be. He knew what he should wish for: world peace, homes for the homeless. He knew what he might have asked for himself before tonight: a place on the debate team at school that fall or, better yet, a starting position on the football team, anything that would make his father proud of him for once. Or maybe he should ask for something important but more personal, like that his new baby brother or sister be born healthy. But when Fischer looked down at the Stone glowing in his palm, it was all he really wanted.

"What are you waiting for?" David asked. "A burning bush? Just make a wish."

"Okay, okay." Fischer held the last Stone. "I wish for . . ." But just as his eyes closed and he opened his mouth to speak, his mind erupted with its own thought. *Thistle.*

"Well, go on," David prompted.

"Bring me . . ." *Thistle. Thistle.* The Stone dropped from

his hand and into the flames. "Thistle," he whispered, then drew back in surprise at having said the name out loud.

"What was that?" David asked. "Because for one incredible moment I could have sworn that you said whistle. And not even you, Fish Head, would waste the extreme outside possibility of a real wish coming true on something that *stupid*."

Fischer wasn't up to fending off David's persistent attempts to make him feel foolish. He was shaken and exhausted.

"I'll tell you what I wished for if I get it," he said. "But right now, I'm going to bed." He knew what Grandpa would say: "Why do you let David get under your skin?" He recalled Grandpa's loss with familiar pain, wished for the umpteenth time that this summer visit were over, then picked up the coffee can to hide away on the shelves. With his luck, Aunt Kathy would come downstairs tomorrow, smell telltale smoke from the fire, and somehow find this can. He plunged his hand into the coffee can, eager to touch the smooth, warm Stones again, but there was nothing there, just the powdery smoothness of ash. He felt dread rising, felt the blood rush from his face and leave him cold and empty. Where were the Stones?

David struck another match.

"Something's happened." Fischer tried to hide his alarm. "The Stones are gone."

"Gone!" David snatched the coffee can and shook it.

"They can't be. Why would they suddenly disappear now?" He shrugged as they started back up the stairs. "Oh, well. Hey, nothing gained, nothing lost. Easy come, easy go. Right, Fish Head?" At the top of the stairs he retreated to his own room.

Fischer shucked his T-shirt and jeans and draped them on his bedpost before he dropped onto his bed. Gone. The Stones were gone. A giant moon spied at him through the shutters as he fell into a restless sleep.

He dreamed that he was home, that something terrible was happening although he wasn't sure what it was. He ran to Grandpa's house and burst in through the front door. Amazingly, Grandpa was alive, looking at the sports page at his breakfast table and drinking his usual first-thing-in-the-morning root beer from the can. He pushed back his chair and took a long swig of his soda. Then, looking Fischer straight in the eye, he told him, "Don't worry, sport, I'm right here with you. Got it? Though I walk through the valley of the shadow of death, I shall fear no evil."

I shall fear no evil. I shall fear no evil.

Fischer thought that perhaps he had awoken, but then he lay back. He must still be dreaming. He could think of no other explanation for the face forming before him, pale and luminous as moonlight.

/ / /

Hey, now! All you night owls, thanks for tuning in to WBST, your late-night, all-night radio station, where we keep you up on all that's happening when it's happening in Atlanta, Kennesaw, White Horse, and our surrounding listener areas. . . .

If you still have one eye open, listen up, folks. Don't want to put a damper on your spirits, but just heard some news regarding that wonderful weekend weather we promised you earlier this evening. Seems El Niño had some plans of his own. Clouds have rolled into our area. Outside the station there's a fog as thick as Granny's gravy, if you know what I'm saying. I have reports of some light rain west of Chattanooga. You'll be seeing it in Kennesaw and White Horse by early morning, and that's probably not good news for our morning commuters. So set your alarms fifteen minutes early. You can sleep in Saturday. And hey, if you've got to get up and head in to work tomorrow morning, let me ask you something. What are you still doing up?

/ / /

CHAPTER THREE

There was a time when Clarence Mittelstadt could sleep the whole night through and wake in the morning to the sound of the alarm still feeling fatigued. But that was ages ago, when he was a very young man working overtime at the Dodge factory in Detroit. Now his body seemed to have discarded its need for sleep much as someone might lose his taste for sweets or red meat.

A few hours ago, at nine, he had gone to bed exhausted, slept soundly, then snapped to attention. At eleven-thirty he quit staring at the ceiling, rolled himself out of bed, and walked barefoot to his den. His wife, Mary Anne, would not have let him get away with that.

"Sorry, Mary," he said out loud as he sprawled across the sofa and clicked on the TV.

She'd bought him a pair of sheepskin slippers last year, three months before she went into cardiac arrest one afternoon and died, leaving him alone in the house they had shared for thirty-something years. Without her to please, Clarence had taken to leaving the slippers on the floor of his closet, where they attracted clumps of dust, same as his work shoes and his good white bucks.

By eleven forty-five Clarence had come to the conclusion that nothing was worse than the late-night news, and by midnight he'd skimmed the latest *Outdoor Life* and *Popular Mechanics* magazines his daughter, Beth, subscribed to for him. By one o'clock he had beaten himself at a game of checkers and sat down at the front window to listen to his favorite late-night talk show on the radio, sipping a mug of warm milk and hoping that unlike other evenings, it might work its magic and lull him back to sleep.

Outside the window a gigantic wagon wheel moon lighted the landscape. As though he were an artist, Clarence held his thumb up to measure it. Almost five fingers across. He hadn't seen a moon like that since one night when he had been a midshipman in the navy. Come to think of it, that was the kind of moon riding the skies the night his ship was hit by an enemy torpedo and sunk, leaving him foundering in a life raft for almost three days.

Just yesterday Beth had called and asked him to consider moving into an apartment at the new retirement place near her house. She hinted that his mind was not as sharp as it once had been. If that were true, then how could he remember that night so long ago?

Now a figure appeared against the girth of the moon. Whoever it was stopped, framed in a white circle of light, and looked down onto his street from the top of Hailey Hill. The figure was in silhouette, but Clarence knew at once it was a man by his lean, straight body and wide-legged stance. Something flapped out behind him, and Clarence guessed it was a coat, though why someone would wear such a thing on a warm summer night, he had no earthly idea. On his head was a wide-brimmed hat.

Clarence leaned forward slightly, watching as the man began down the hill. Only the top of him, from midsection up, remained visible against the moon, then only his head, then no part of him at all. The mottled surface of the moon was empty again, save for the clouds that suddenly rolled over it. Clarence put the TV on mute and turned up the radio.

"Well, do you think the tornadoes that touched down tonight have been precipitated by recent changes in weather?" the radio voice was asking. *"How else would you explain the rash of tornadoes, and storms, and flooding, and earthquakes and all the rest?"*

"Why, the fulfillment of prophecy," the guest said. *"The end times."*

Clarence watched his window. He didn't like to hear talk like that. It disturbed him, not for himself—his own time was near enough—but for his daughter and her husband and his new grandbaby, Mindy.

Down the street, way past the sycamores planted in the median, beyond the streetlight at the end of their block, Clarence detected a moving shadow.

"*Nobody knows when the end will come,*" the host of the talk show said.

"*That's certainly true, but we must be the watchmen. We must look for the signs. 'For nation shall rise against nation,*'" the man quoted, "*'and kingdom against kingdom: and there shall be famines, and pestilences, and earthquakes in divers places. All these are the beginning of sorrows.'*"

The host paused. "*But what about later in that same Book of Matthew, sir? 'But of that day and hour knoweth no man, no, not the angels of heaven, but my Father only.'*"

"*Well, I guess we could sit here swapping verses all night if that's what you want to do,*" the guest said.

The host laughed. Uncomfortably, Clarence thought.

When he glanced back again to the window, he saw the man in the wide-brimmed hat standing under the streetlamp. Above him beetles seemed to swim in a pool of light. He couldn't be up to much good, lurking about so late at night. What was he doing? Clarence wondered. He had half a mind to call the authorities.

Armed with his remote phone, he ducked under the window and peered out into the night again. The man was still there. Rain began to fall through the aura of light that surrounded the lamppost. The fellow didn't pull his coat around him. He seemed to be interested only in observing the line of houses. Finally he started walking toward Elise Donatelli's house across the street. He seemed oblivious of the rain as it became sheets and drummed on the sidewalk.

Clarence clicked off the television. He was having a hard time following the man's progress in the driving rain, but then he saw him appear at the top of Elise's stoop, peer into her house through her Dutch door, and ring the doorbell. Now he really would call the police, Clarence thought, squeezing the phone in his hand. He was about to dial when he heard the talk show host asking, *"What are the so-called other signs of the end?"*

"False prophets," the guest answered. *"Performing miracles and using their powers of deception."*

"Ah, well, we see plenty of that these days."

"You bet," the talk show guest said. *"You bet we do. And it's just the beginning."*

A light came on in Elise's front hall, and Clarence could see her making her way down the stairs and into her lit foyer. Her hair was wrapped in those funny curlers no one wore anymore.

"Don't open your door, Elise," Clarence whispered.

Elise opened her door, but only slightly. Clarence guessed that her safety chain was attached.

He could not see how the man greeted Elise. He could only see the man's back, and not much of it at that, with that long, black coat flapping. The man swept his hat from his head in the kind of cordial fashion that had vanished with carriages and bustles.

Elise shook her head, her hand clenching the wad of material at the neck of her bathrobe.

Clarence stood. He dialed 9, then 1, then—

Elise closed her door and shut off her foyer light, then her porch lamp, but not before the man turned suddenly and smiled straight across from Elise's stoop to the place where Clarence stood with the phone in his hand. The phone clattered as it hit the floor.

Oh, no, Clarence thought. He dropped to his knees to grope around in the darkness.

"So what you're actually saying, Dr. M, is what? Give up? We're all doomed anyway?"

"No, no, of course not," the guest said. *"I'm saying, 'Get your heart in a purer state. Recognize evil when you see it.' Chances are you'll find it inside yourself."*

Clarence heard his doorbell ring. He had found the phone under the coffee table. He waited a moment and pushed in the 9 again, but calling the emergency number now seemed like overkill. After all, the stranger had done nothing wrong, only gone to Elise's house and left without incident.

The doorbell rang again. The man wasn't going away. Clarence stood, stared toward the hallway, then walked to the front door. He wasn't about to open it, but suddenly it seemed he wanted to. He opened the door a hair more than Elise had.

This time the man did not lift his hat, only pinched the brim of it, allowing water from the rain to drip down. "Sorry to bother you so late, friend," the man said. His skin was devoid of lines, even his hands. Clarence's own hand gripping the door was raised with corded veins and brown with liver spots. "I'm looking for something, and I wonder if you could help me?"

Clarence's palms went sweaty on the doorframe. "What might that be?"

"Well, it's two boys," the man said. His eyes flickered up to Clarence's. They were bright red pinpoints.

"Wha—" Clarence muttered. Fear had sprung up, loud and clanging, but as he stared into the man's eyes, his body seemed to forget the actions that corresponded to terror.

"Two boys who live in this area have been very naughty, I'm afraid," the man said. "But you're not a naughty boy, are you, Clarence?"

Clarence shook his head.

"So you know what a problem it is to have bad boys around. You wouldn't want them in your neighborhood, would you?" The man gestured toward the tidy front yards of the houses. "Not after you've lived here so long. Why, I bet you know everybody on this street."

Clarence nodded.

"These boys are about fourteen, fifteen," the man said.

"Just the age when they start getting in a bit of trouble and it winds up ending . . . badly. Well, that's just the sort of trouble these boys have gotten into."

Clarence clucked his tongue. "Bad," he said.

"Oh, yes, they are, they are." The man nodded. "And that's why I wonder if you might point me in their direction."

Behind Clarence the radio blared on.

"We have to make choices about our own behavior, is that it in a nutshell, sir?" the host said.

"Absolutely. We have free will. We can resist temptation, resist evil. But first we have to know what it looks like."

Clarence blinked his eyes. I have free will, he thought. Resist temptation. "I don't know two boys like that living on this street," he said.

The man looked at him as though he didn't believe him. "One is tall and dark with broad shoulders, and the other is . . . well, he's more a crafty lad than one might imagine. As tall as the other, but lighter-haired, and spare."

Clarence's hands were trembling. Something told him it was important not to look into the man's eyes. His head began to pound as he shifted his focus ever so slightly to the right. Now, he could hear his own thoughts clearly again, not just the ones the man seemed to want inside his head. His heart began pounding like a jackhammer.

"Do you know the boys I mean?" the stranger asked.

Clarence tried not to think of David Talbot and his cousin Fischer playing football on the front lawn of their yellow house. He could see them, stopping to raise a hand in greeting as he drove by in his Buick and tapped the horn. Clarence blinked his eyes, and the image disappeared. He had the feeling the stranger would like to reach in, grab a handful of his thoughts, pop them into his mouth, chew and swallow them down like popcorn.

"I don't know anyone like that living on this street," Clarence said.

The man took a step backward into the rain as if to go. "Then I suppose you can't help me tonight." The red dots in his eyes disappeared into dark brown orbs. He turned to go; then suddenly he stopped and looked back at Clarence, still standing at the door.

"What is it, Clarence?" the man asked.

Clarence heard his own breath racing in and out of him. He felt his teeth clench with conviction. All his days as a youth in church came flooding back to him. "I know you," he said.

The man cocked his head. "Well, well." For a moment he seemed to shrink away. "Not many do anymore. I admire that." The man nodded at Clarence's house. "You don't have long left here," he said. "And I could use a clever man like you, Clarence." He clasped his hands behind him. "You've heard that marvelous saying? A few good men?"

"Much obliged," Clarence said, his breath ragged with fear. "But I have other plans." He slammed the door, locked it, and slid to the floor.

A moment later Clarence staggered into his living room and looked out the window again. The man was strolling down the road. Lightning flashed, then struck a tree, sending sparks flying from the streetlamp. The man turned in the road and waggled his finger as though he could see Clarence watching him from below the sill. Then he disappeared into the shadows.

Clarence forgot all about the radio as he hurried down the hallway to find his slippers and pull them on. "How was that, Mary?" he whispered into the darkness.

The night is far spent, the day is at hand:
let us therefore cast off the works of
darkness, and let us put on the armor
of light. —*Romans 13:12*

CHAPTER FOUR

Fischer felt as though he had no more closed his eyes than a hand was shaking him awake. "Funny, Fischer," David said. "Okay, hilarious, in fact."

Fischer opened his eyes to see David stooped over him in his white Jockeys, holding what Grandpa and all his friends at the Kiwanis's annual pancake breakfast used to tell him never to take: an actual wooden nickel.

"Under my pillow. Adorable. Just like the tooth fairy."

But Fischer stared past David. There, seated in his corner chair, was something much stranger: a boy, the flame maker from the campfire. The boy was still dressed in his long, dirty coat and squashed hat, but in the dim light of dawn Fischer saw what he had not seen the night before. The boy's smudged face was a soft oval, his eyes large and dark with anger. He removed his hat, and hair as pale as oxeye daisies fell from underneath, dropping in waves past his collarbones.

David turned and scrambled backward onto the bed, yanking the sheet away to cover himself. It was then that Fischer recognized what he should have from the first: This stranger, the one who had awoken when Fischer had stolen the Stones the night before, was no boy. He was a girl, no older than Fischer himself.

The girl rose slowly, her eyes affixed to Fischer's face. "What trickery is this, Belial? Do what you're about, and spare me further insult."

"Who are you?" Fischer asked, though something about the girl was familiar.

The girl placed her fingers, clad with silver rings, against her hips.

"You more than any other would know my name, Deceiver, for I am from dust. Let me assure you, this may be my end, but Solomon lives, and another Keeper will replace me. Remember my name, for it will confound your sleep and bloody your memory henceforth." She took a step toward Fischer, and he jumped up, all nerves and adrenaline, ready to bolt from the room.

The girl stretched out her arm and pointed at him as though she were lining up an arrow in a bow. "Remember me long, Belial. Remember Thistle!"

"What's going on?" David asked Fischer, who stared dumbstruck at the girl across the room. Despite her slight frame, she appeared fierce as a warrior. "What's thistle?"

Through the open window the clank of metal cans hitting the sidewalk was followed by a yawning creak, the roar of the garbage truck, and then only the persistent yapping of a dog.

The girl's eyes narrowed, and she began to pace. "*I* am Thistle, as well you know. Belial, show yourself at once. This cat-and-mouse fancy is for the young, and I am far too old for such games."

"Do you know this girl?" David asked.

Fischer was afraid to answer. He didn't know the girl, but somehow he felt he did. Or was it only his memory of the Stone in the dark and then his thought: *Thistle.*

"Wait a sec, wait a sec." David snapped his fingers and pointed. "It's the short kid from the campfire."

The room became silent as each party studied the other. Then all at once Thistle stomped a muddy bootheel onto the floorboards. "Impossible!"

"David," his mother called up the stairs, "no rough-housing. It's too early for that, do you hear me?"

"If you are not Belial, then who are you? And where are the Stones?" The girl folded her arms. "Fools! Heaven help me! I am in the midst of imbeciles!" She snapped the curtains together. Turning to Fischer with a face paper white with anger, she asked with visible restraint, "What have you done with the Stones?"

David stared accusingly at Fischer.

"You're in this, too," Fischer said. "Remember? Aladdin?"

"Enough! We must undo what you have done. Give me the remaining Stones at once."

David thumped Fischer on the back. "If you have any, give them to her now. My mother will kill us if she finds out there's a girl up here."

"We only had two Stones," Fischer said, "and those are essentially . . . well, gone."

The girl stared, incredulous. "Gone? Tell me at once how you used them."

"David asked for money."

"And received it?" the girl asked.

David held up the wooden nickel.

The girl scoffed. "Fool's gold. Sent only to rebuke you."

She regarded Fischer with curiosity before turning her attention back to David. "But your wooden coin tells me something of you, boy. You see, the Stones return to each owner a share of himself. And for that reason I would presume you are a jokester, a comic of sorts, or so you would have us imagine. Though I confess that so far you do not strike me funny in the least. And you"—she directed these words to Fischer—"you used the other Stone, did you not?"

"Yes," Fischer admitted.

"So." She walked a full circle around him. "If I am delivered into your hands, then what share of yourself would that reveal?"

"I have no idea. I used one of your Stones, yes, and I spoke your name, true, but—"

"You spoke her name?" David appeared incredulous. "Do you know her?"

"No," Fischer insisted. "I have no clue who she is. And I'd like to know how she got in the house. Look, if it's the Stones you're after, I'm sorry, they're gone."

"You used them without thought of consequence," the girl said.

"I won't argue that," Fischer said. "And I shouldn't have, but now that it's done . . . I'll pay you back."

"Oh, you will. But not in the way of your meaning. And the payment will extend far beyond all of us. You have no idea what you have begun, but let me try, as they say in these times, to paint you the picture." She turned again to the curtain and yanked one side open. "Observe."

Over the top of the church spire, gray clouds were rolling across the pale sky like fragments of metal arranged with a magnetic wand.

"So? It's going to rain," David said, hopping over to Fischer's drawer and grabbing out a pair of shorts and a T-shirt. "What's the big deal?"

Thistle dropped the fabric of the curtain as David pulled on his shorts.

"Ah, yes, it will rain, feeble mind. But the rain will become torrents that rise over these houses. And then the winds will whirl and carry away your villages, and the earth will open and swallow you whole."

David pulled his T-shirt over his head. "Look, we took your stones, Miss whoever-you-are." David finger-combed his hair in swipes. "And now you're riled. Understandably. But don't you think you might be overreacting?"

Thistle turned to Fischer. "You were my caller, the Taker of the Stones, were you not?"

Fischer tried to avoid looking into her eyes. It was a ploy he had learned from his father, one his dad used every time he left home for his next destination. "Yes, I took them."

David slammed his hand against the doorframe. "Don't admit anything, Fischer. My dad has an attorney—"

"What's going on up there, David?" Uncle Matthew's voice floated up from below.

"Nothing, Dad!"

"Look, this was an accident," Fischer whispered. "We were at the campfire. We took your Stones—"

"He took," David interrupted.

"But I've never done anything like that before in my life."

"Is that true?" She stopped short with eyes bright with tears. "Well, I believe you will soon wish you had let this occasion pass as well. For you cannot conceive the depth and breadth of your error. And without another Stone none of this can be undone. Now that Belial knows a

Taker has acted, God have mercy on the Keepers. On all of us," she said, eyeing Fischer. "For you look no more able than a babe in arms."

"Now hold on a second," Fischer said. "Wait a minute. Keepers, Takers. What are they?"

"We Keepers are the two who protect the Stones, but why do I explain? It will mean nothing to you."

"You're so right." David leaned against the edge of the desk.

"Your minds are weak and tainted. You know nothing of questing. Nothing of honor. Why the two of you are just common thieves."

Again, a call came up from below. "Fischer, David, breakfast. I'm going to be late to work if you don't hurry up."

Fischer looked at David in panic. What if Aunt Kathy came upstairs?

"I'll try to get Mom and Dad out of the house and off to work. Then I'm going down to the basement to see if by some miracle, the Stones are still there." David turned to leave the room. "In the meantime, she's got to go, Fish, I mean it."

David slipped into the hall and closed the door behind him. Fischer turned the lock, then found some clothes in the dresser drawer. He shuffled into the closet with his quilt around him and yanked on shorts and a T-shirt, but Thistle didn't even seem to notice he was gone.

"He does not understand."

Fischer peered out from behind the closet door. The girl stood with her hands clasped behind her back, staring out past the darkening sky, beyond the branches to the hill where the moon had appeared only hours earlier.

"Who doesn't understand?" Fischer emerged from the closet and threw his quilt onto his bed. "David, you mean?"

"David," Thistle said. "And you are of what name?"

"Fischer."

Thistle grabbed his hand, and though Fischer tried to wrench away, the girl held his wrist tighter. "Listen well, Fischer. Whether or not it was your intent, you are the Taker. You are the one who must return me to my rightful place."

"No problem." Fischer's face was burning, and he wanted to run from the room, but he knew he couldn't. He had been at the girl's campfire. He had taken her Stones. Now she had shown up with her wild stories about Keepers and Takers. But no matter who she was, how strange she sounded, he owed her something for what he'd done. "I'll take you back to your campsite as soon as my aunt and uncle leave for work."

"No, no," Thistle said. "My father is no longer there."

Perfect, Fischer thought. Now the man he'd taken the Stones from was this girl's father.

"We left that place late in the night. There was a great

commotion, a chase, and then we ran and jumped into the empty belly of the train. He must be hours away by now."

Fischer's mind was racing. "Okay, that complicates things, but don't worry, I can still get you back to your father. Where were you headed?"

"He—we were headed," Thistle said, releasing Fischer's hand, "as leaves blow."

Fischer frowned. "I don't get it."

"Solomon and I have no real home or destination. This we do for the sake of the Stones, but that is another matter. But how will Solomon know what has become of me? We were traveling north, asleep when I was tumbled into a vortex of darkness, as if some nightmare had taken hold of me. By now he has most likely awoken and found me and the Stones missing."

"But that's great news," Fischer said, suddenly renewed with hope. "He'll come looking for you."

"No, that is not the way of things. He must continue. He carries the Stones. Solomon is the First Keeper, and I am the Second. Separated from him, I will soon be helpless as a butterfly in a beetle's jaws. He knows, and I know as well, that already Belial seeks me out to destroy me."

"Destroy you?" Fischer asked. "Who is this guy?"

"And you will die, too, Fischer. As well as your friend David and everyone you know. We will all perish for this tragic error."

Suddenly Fischer's thoughts jumped to his father far

away. His mother at home, waiting for the birth of his new brother or sister. Fear shot through him. He rubbed his arms, tense under the sleeves of his T-shirt, and studied the girl before him. No matter what his instincts told him, he couldn't have known her before. She was clearly insane.

"I believe that you *think* that's what will happen," he said. "But I promise, no one is going to die. Tell me who you are, you and your father."

"I will tell you what I can, as you wish, but know this, all else who witnessed the saga are long dead. So hear me well. For time escapes us even now."

Fischer walked over to the window. The back of his neck tingled as raindrops began to pelt the glass of his room.

"Wait." He didn't really want to know any more. He should keep his distance from this crazy girl instead of inviting himself further into her life. "Do you want anything? A bagel and orange juice, maybe?"

"A glass of wine, perhaps." Thistle shucked her coat and laid it on the floor, revealing a rough blue shirt cinched with a heavy leather belt to which a silver scabbard was attached.

Fischer was suddenly light-headed. "Maybe we'd better just stick to the story."

Thistle sat cross-legged on the floor. Her hair fell over her shoulders like the silk tassels that held back Aunt Kathy's curtains, and Fischer felt himself hold his breath as she raised her eyes, blue as deep water, to his. "It begins five centuries ago."

Fischer sank down onto the bed and listened to the rhythm of rain increase on the roof outside. This was going to take a lot longer than he had thought.

/ / /

The Weather Channel
White Horse, Georgia
July 12
8:00 A.M.

Light rain, becoming heavier during the afternoon and
into the evening. More rain tomorrow, through the night,
and predicted to extend throughout our five-day forecast.
Temperature at the Atlanta airport, an unseasonably cool
seventy-six degrees.

/ / /

How then shall they call on him in whom
they have not believed? And how shall
they believe in him of whom they have
not heard? —*Romans 10:14*

CHAPTER FIVE

"Start with how you got here." Fischer propped his chin on his hand. "You followed us, didn't you, or did the man that chased me into the woods tell you where to find me?"

"Solomon and I do not travel with companions," Thistle said, her eyes flickering over him. "Though it seems that now, without my consent, that, too, will change."

Fischer ignored this comment. "Well, whoever the guy was, he seemed to know I had something that he wanted."

"Yes, Belial wastes little time." Thistle rose and went to his desk, where she selected a piece of quartz from a box of rocks he had begun collecting summers ago. She seemed unaware that Fischer was there as she put the rock back and began to pick up other things. A flashlight, a recent letter from his father, a Swiss Army knife. "Are these your belongings?" She glanced at the title of the book Fischer had been reading. "*Primitive Civilizations.* So you are a scholar."

"Hardly. But I do like history."

The girl turned to him, eyes sparkling. "If it's history you love, then I have seen enough of that to satisfy many scholars. And the Stones are precisely that, history. You must help me return to Solomon or he will travel on without me, in search of my successor, the next Keeper."

"He wouldn't," Fischer said.

Thistle held up a hand. "He would, as I would, for the sake of the Stones." She hesitated as though she were carefully selecting her words. "You see, the Stones are about everything good in this world, and how strong, yet fragile, that good can be."

"I don't understand," Fischer said.

"Ah, it will be difficult to explain. People today have a narrow view of the past."

"Not the people I know." Again, Fischer felt as if his life were on display as the girl wandered around his room. "My mother is an archaeologist, Native American culture; the past is her whole life. I've slogged through tombs, sites, the works, as long as I can remember."

"But what about the past that is not found in such places? What about the past that continues to live inside each of us? What do you know of that?"

Suddenly Fischer was standing alone back in the museum in Leeland, Stevie Ray blaring, and something beginning to thaw inside him.

"The Stones have much to do with believing in things that can no longer be seen, Fischer."

Maybe that was true, Fischer thought as Thistle picked up his T-shirt scribbled with faded Egyptian hieroglyphics, then dropped it into a pile on his desk. Because even though Thistle was standing right in front of him, he was still having a hard time believing she was real.

"Listen to me, boy. I speak of the holy nature of the Stones. Of how I came to be here." Thistle turned to study a movie poster of *The Lost World.* "You, Fischer, after taking the Stones, called me for whatever reason and brought me here to you."

"Brought, as in conjured?" Fischer stood quickly and looked nervously around the room. "Come on."

The girl continued to stare at him.

"Okay, let's say that I did, I brought you here," he said. "There were plenty of other Stones in your father's pouch. He could just call you back himself. Why do you need me?"

"Solomon's Stones lost their power when you took the ones you did. Only the Taker's Stones possess power now. If the Taker's Stones have all been used, as you say they have, then the Stones in Solomon's pouch would have regained their strength in full, and he would have returned me to his side. But I am not with Solomon, am I? And why is that?" Thistle demanded.

"I don't know." Fischer was feeling attacked. "Tell me."

The girl's eyes smoldered. "Because the Taker still *has* the Stones."

"No. I told you what we did with them. They're gone."

"I suspect you know more than you tell," Thistle shot back. "Because you desire the Stones yourself. You took them once last night. Why should I believe that you are above keeping others secret?"

"I'm not like that." But Fischer could see it was futile. She didn't know him any more than he knew her.

"When I tell you that you conjured me here," Thistle said, "your mind, doubtless, races to thoughts of magic and illusions. The matters of which we speak are of far graver importance."

"Like miracles, maybe?" Fischer shook his head and sat on his desktop. "I'd like to believe in miracles, really. I used to have this conversation with my grandfather all the time, but the truth is, miracles are defunct, antiquated."

Fischer remembered one of his last debates with Grandpa. When Fischer had started to scrutinize the idea of heaven, Grandpa held up his hand, picked up his empty plate from dinner, and pushed himself back from the table. "Some things you've got to have the courage to trust," he'd said flatly. Then he'd made a face as if to say "take it or leave it," pulled on his hat, and had gone outside to water the lawn.

"Miracles are extinct, like the dinosaurs in that poster," Fischer said.

Thistle's expression was serious. "If that is your belief, then I must try to appeal to you in some other way to take me to Solomon. For I have no evidence. Nothing to read or examine. If you do not have the courage to trust, then I cannot make you believe otherwise."

Her words, so much like Grandpa's, caught Fischer off guard. He was suddenly speechless.

Thistle picked up his CD player. "I have seen these devices. They make music, do they not? Yet I see no musicians, no singers. How do you know that the music you hear is not something you have made up within your own imagination."

"Because that's technology. And yes, computers, CD players, even telephones—those are today's miracles."

"Wondrous, yes. Because they began with someone believing not only in himself but beyond. Isn't there something, Fischer, that you can't fully comprehend but know to be real?"

Fischer looked at his bare feet. Yes, there was something. His dreams. But he wasn't sure that dreams should be considered real.

"You have to feel it within you, Fischer. I need you to help me find Solomon. It is the only hope that this may end well. Without you, neither Solomon nor I shall survive. Perhaps when I am gone, you can convince yourself that I never existed. Then you can go back to believing in your miracles," she said, holding up his CD player. "Till Belial takes them away."

The door cracked open, and David slipped inside the room. "Finally. They left for work. And if anyone was wondering, the Stones are gone, kaput. So . . ." He looked from Thistle to Fischer. "Have we solved our little problem?"

Fischer glared at him, but David did not seem to notice.

"I saved your hide, Fish," he said. "I told Mom you weren't feeling great. She thinks you've got some stomach thing. But that won't last forever. Eventually she's going to know something's up." He nodded to Thistle. "So how about getting her out of here before the folks get home this afternoon?"

"I'm working on it, David, but . . . " Fischer opened his mouth but could not imagine what he could say to make David believe any of what had passed between him and the girl. "It's complicated."

"Complicated how?" David asked.

Lightning flashed in the window and froze their figures against the wall.

"Well, for starters, she thinks I should take her back to her father. Because of the Stones."

"Okay," David told Thistle. He scrutinized his image in the mirror. "We can do that. We go back to the campfire, find your father, then you go your way and we'll go ours."

Thistle spoke in a stern voice. "You can go back, but you'll find no fire. You can look for my father, but you will find no one. He has long departed."

David dropped backward onto the bed. "Just perfect."

"Wait. You must have had some kind of backup plan," Fischer said. "You know, like David and me, we used to have this system. If one of us got lost when we were out in the woods, the other knew to go to a certain place, this tree, and that's where we'd stay till the lost guy showed up."

"Yes." Thistle pushed her hair away from her face. "I do recall such a plan, though it was long ago that we last spoke of it."

"It doesn't matter," David said. "Your father wouldn't forget something like that."

Fischer felt relief flood through him; then he remembered his own father. Still, David was right. Most fathers were more conscientious about their children than Fischer's. "Where is this meeting place? Let's go. Now. While we can."

"Where are you supposed to meet your old man?" David asked. "Time's a-wasting."

Thistle walked over to the desk, where an inflatable globe dangled from kite string, a relic of Fischer's own past. "His thinking was this: No matter what the township or kingdom or country, the exact center was our appointed meeting place."

"The exact center?" Fischer asked.

David thumped the globe with his index finger. "This just gets better all the time."

Thistle shook her head. "We have seen capitals rise and fall; we have seen the ruin of many nations. What Solomon said was the center of the place. And he is a man of plain words."

Fischer stole a look at Thistle.

"The exact center of the United States." David studied the globe. "You're the resident genius, Fish Head. Just for laughs, where would that be?"

"I don't know," he said. Suddenly, like the times when he was alone in the museum, something inside Fischer had begun to shift like plates of rock. This Thistle, this girl, seemed so familiar to him—why? Shaken, he stood and turned away, hoping to avoid her eyes. But a moment later, when he looked up to glimpse her reflection in the mirror, he found her staring back at him. Though her expression was nothing like his own, more perplexed than amazed, he read it clearly. Why? it asked simply, echoing his own thoughts. And then something further: Why you?

. . . Setteth it on a candlestick, that they which enter in may see the light.

—*Luke 8:16*

CHAPTER SIX

The sounds of falling rain made the remnants of breakfast scattered across the kitchen table seem all the more dismal. Fischer had gone back to the woods, looked along the path and on the banks of the stream, hoping to find a lost Stone, but he'd returned empty-handed. Now he and David silently studied Thistle, who, having gorged herself on bananas, bagels with jam and cream cheese to spare, had begun to inspect the contents of the refrigerator and the pantry.

"Let's go through this one more time," David said. "Somehow we called you away from your father. And now, because Fischer took your Stones, you want him to take you to this place where your father has said he will meet you, which just happens to be the center of the United States."

"Precisely." Thistle nodded and closed the refrigerator

door. "And we must meet him before three nights have fallen or he will travel on without me."

"Fischer, can I see you a minute?" David pushed back from the table and nodded in the direction of the hallway.

They left Thistle in the kitchen, rummaging through drawers.

"Fischer, let's get serious," David said. "The girl obviously has a screw loose."

"I know, I know, it does sound impossible, but—"

"But what? Look, Fischer, she's becoming a gigantic problem."

Fischer looked back toward the kitchen. The girl's story was like his dreams. He knew there was something important there, but he couldn't put his finger on what it was. "For some reason I think that maybe we should help her. Or at least think about it."

"You see, that's it. Right there. You're caught up, and for the life of me, I can't figure why." David cast Fischer a dark look Fischer knew well enough to translate. Another week with hopeless Fischer. "You're usually so practical. So confess, Fish. Tell me you're not getting hooked in by Miss Unlikely."

"No, it's nothing like that." But he knew there was no chance that David would understand. Through the side-lights of the front door, he watched the top branches of the great, lush oak in the front yard strain in the wind.

"Still, you've got to admit, she's not your average girl. And there are things I can't explain. Like the wooden nickel under your pillow. And her being here."

"I wished for money, not some wooden slug. And how about her little speech in your room, that 'return a share of yourself' routine? Oh, yeah, very smooth." David pulled Fischer farther away from the kitchen. "As far as how she got here, maybe she saw us sneak out and followed us back to the house. She might be some runaway, some vagrant looking for a handout. Maybe she's duping us, or you at least. Have you considered that?"

Fischer had, but the more he thought about it, the more the girl seemed totally unable to be anything but honest.

"Are you sure you looked everywhere for her stupid Stones?" David asked.

"Everywhere. And I didn't find anything," Fischer said.

"Well, she has to go. That's all there is to it."

"Be reasonable, David," Fischer said. "I can't just open the door and put her out. And even if I did, she wouldn't go. She's convinced I'm this Taker, that somehow I can get her back to her father."

David frowned. "You're even starting to sound like her. Before we do anything else, I'll search our computer encyclopedia. Try to find out where the exact center of the United States is. If it isn't too far, maybe we can talk her into an alternate means of transportation, like the bus. Otherwise, concentrate on getting her out of here before she causes any more trouble. Got it?"

"Fine." Fischer turned toward the kitchen. "Hey, something's burning," he shouted.

David bolted from the hallway with Fischer on his heels. They darted around the corner and nearly fell into Thistle, who sat on the floor, holding a lit match over a tea candle.

"What's all this?" David asked.

"I must look into the future and read it as well as I am able," she said as she brought the match to the candlewick. "I must see my hope. Or my fate." The flame caught. "It is better to know, to prepare for what lies ahead."

As Fischer edged down on the floor across from Thistle, he wondered what would have happened if he hadn't wished on the Stone and if Thistle hadn't come when he had. Certainly his life would be less complicated now, but he also would not have met her, and a part of him objected to that.

A tiny green light flickered in Thistle's eyes. "I see the hare."

David stretched out on the floor and propped his head on his hand. Behind him, the faucet leaked fat drops that lengthened before falling into a pot in the sink.

"The rabbit." Thistle squinted with effort. "One among us is known for his timidity."

Fischer avoided David's eyes.

"Now I spy an hourglass. The sign of racing time and—"
Thistle's voice halted. "The owl," she whispered. "An
omen. Dark days lie ahead."

"And?" Fischer said.

Thistle's eyes widened. "A fire within the fire." Her
breathing was quick, and her voice thin as a wisp. "This
denotes earthly disturbances to come. I have seen this sign
only once in the beginning of the last century. A terrible,
tragic time when a double-tailed comet marked the death
of a Keeper struck down by evil."

Fischer looked up sharply.

"Then earthquakes and violent skies and strange occur-
rences followed."

David stared into the flame as though he might discover
something there. When Fischer caught his eye, he shook
his head in obvious disbelief.

"The Hawk!" Thistle rubbed her hands together as
though they were cold. "He comes!"

For a moment Fischer thought he felt the shuddering of
Thistle's body in the planks under his feet. "What's the
Hawk?"

"Belial, the Evil One—he now has knowledge that I am
parted from Solomon."

"Enough!" David suddenly blew out the flame and
stood. "Look, Miss whoever-you-are, I'm through with
party games. So let's get this straight: You can't stay here. I
don't know what you're after, but—"

"Fool!" Thistle leaped to her feet but dropped again as her knees gave way beneath her.

"Are you all right?" Fischer crouched beside her. He searched David's eyes over her head but only found doubt.

"I must be more weary than I imagined," Thistle said. "I only wish I knew how Solomon fares."

"Look, I was going to tell you. We have good news." Fischer was afraid that if Thistle persisted a moment longer, David would banish her into the rain before he could figure out a plan. "David had this idea about finding the center of the United States on his computer."

Thistle pulled herself up resignedly. "One of the miracles you believe in."

"In the meantime, we should find her something else to wear." David looked Thistle over from her tunic and belt to her leather boots. "Down in the basement I think there's a trunk of my Mom's old stuff, Fish. Why don't you have a look?"

David disappeared into Aunt Kathy's office, while Thistle followed Fischer into the hall and down the basement stairs.

At the bottom of the steps Fischer pulled the string that hung from the simple bulb and socket overhead. The room remained dark, and the gray day outside the narrow windows did little to help. Fischer felt his way along Uncle Matt's tool shelf until he located a flashlight. Clicking it on, he held it aloft so that it shone on the countless stacks of boxes and unused furniture that cast strange shadows onto the wall.

"David said it was back in the corner." Fischer moved down a pathway littered with yellowed packing papers.

Thistle scowled as she picked her way through the boxes. "Why can I not wear my own clothes?"

"You'll call attention to yourself," Fischer called back. "You'll be too conspicuous."

He thought of David's earlier suggestion and smiled. He could just imagine Thistle boarding a Greyhound with her boots and scabbard.

Behind a sealed moving carton, he found a rusty green trunk. Wiping dust from the top with the hem of his shirt, he flipped up the latches and lifted the lid. The smell of mothballs and lavender rose as Fischer handed Thistle the flashlight and yanked up a handful of clothes.

He discarded a tie-dye shirt, a prom dress draped in hot pink netting, then a flowered minidress. From the bottom of the trunk, he pulled a multicolored fake fur stole. "I take it back. You'll call more attention to yourself in this stuff than in your own."

"Will this do?" Thistle stood before him in a long blue velvet dress, with only the cuff of her trousers showing beneath the hem. Fischer wanted to look away, but that seemed impossible. Thistle was beautiful, lit from within like the Stones had been when he had shaken them from the pouch. She stood in the filtered light of the dusty basement like a proud medieval princess.

He cleared his throat. "Where did you find that?"

Thistle shrugged and pointed to the box of hanging clothes marked "Costumes. David, 7th Grade Play, Romeo and Juliet."

All at once Fischer stumbled forward with a jolt, and the light behind Thistle's face seemed to waver like a candle flame.

"Something is amiss." She struggled away from the crates. "Quickly. Find your cousin. Tell him he is in danger."

As they made their way up the stairs, the ground shook as though a jet plane had flown dangerously low over the rooftop. A can of paint fell from Uncle Matthew's shelf, and an assortment of screwdrivers rattled their way across his workbench as Fischer and Thistle staggered into the hallway.

"David!" Fischer glanced in the direction of Aunt Kathy's office.

"Tell him it begins. Go!"

As Fischer ran down the hall, a picture of David at his first communion fell from the wall. Fischer fought to keep his balance as he passed the kitchen, where the pots and pans on the counter clacked and rattled, a bizarre processional marching toward the sudsy water of the sink. He pulled himself around the corner of the office and spotted David crouched under the desk. Blood trickled down David's jaw and stained the front of his shirt. Beside him lay a slab of plaster, and above was the hole that had opened when it fell from the ceiling.

"That looks bad." Fischer ducked to inspect the gash in David's forehead.

"It's okay," David said. "Where's the girl?"

Fischer felt slightly sick from the sight of so much blood. "I left her in the hallway."

David slid out from under the desk and balanced himself on his feet. All at once the shaking stopped, allowing a more subtle sound to intercede, a sound that had become like a bass line in a complicated musical piece: that of falling rain.

Fischer hurried to the place where Thistle sat slumped against the wall, her face damp with tears. "Prophecy says that in earlier days, when Belial freely used his wiles to tempt men, a great shaking rocked the world. The earthly disturbances shown by the flame are a sign—" She stopped and looked at David's forehead. "You are injured."

"I'm fine." David dabbed at the wound with the hem of his shirt. "But wait, didn't you see something like that, earthly disturbances, a fire within a fire, didn't you see that in the flame you lit?"

"Yes," Thistle said. "And dark days to come and the Hawk and—"

"Something else?" Fischer asked.

Thistle screwed up her face. "I saw some notion, but what was it? Just before the flame extinguished." She wiped her cheek with the back of her hand. "A bridge!"

"What does a bridge mean?" David asked.

"That I can change the course of this madness. I know I can if only I reach Solomon. I must go to the place, the center of this country. But first—" She opened the top of the tiny pouch that hung from a cord around her neck and brought out a pinch of something that looked like herbs. When she reached for David's forehead, he flinched, but her fingertips found the gash that still bled freely and pressed the stuff against it. "This will help heal you."

David squinted at Thistle as though it were the first time he had seen her clearly. "Wait," he said. "Tell me again. Who exactly are you?"

Fischer heard the change in David's voice. But before he could grasp the meaning of it, Thistle held out her hands as though she could feel vibrations through her fingertips. "It begins again."

The three of them huddled together as Aunt Kathy's porcelain figurines began to rattle on the bric-a-brac shelves overhead. Moments later the brass lamp in the foyer swung like a bell.

"I have spoken only the truth," Thistle said. Plaster sifted from the ceiling as if through a sieve. "Can you not see that the hourglass in the flame has foretold your future as well as mine? Please, you must take me to my father."

Fischer opened his mouth to speak but was silenced by the look on David's face. He had never seen his cousin appear so positively reverent. What had happened? Then Thistle smiled hesitantly, and Fischer knew. It was something he should have predicted. How could he forget David's numerous sojourns into summer romances, the latest only last week when he had convinced Fischer to slip out one night and meet Anne Rone and her friend Jackie down the street? Fischer had wound up trying to make small talk with Jackie about late-night movies and books, while Anne and David disappeared into the cover of night.

"I'll take you." David smiled, his dark eyes shining. "I should have listened earlier, I know. Still, the whole thing with these quakes . . ." But Fischer could see by the way David stared at Thistle that his sudden willingness to believe her story had little to do with earthquakes. David hadn't taken his eyes from her.

Fischer couldn't stand it. He looked away.

"You say you need to meet your father at the center of the United States? Fine, no problem. Somehow, don't ask me how right now, I'll figure out a way to get you there."

Thistle lifted David's hand and pressed it to her pallid cheek as the tremors that shook the house subsided.

"You would do this? Risk yourself?" Then she turned away and dropped David's hand. "But it is no use. Without the Taker, Belial will surely find us before we can even depart."

"You've got Fischer all wrong." David sent Fischer a meaningful glance as he swept dust from the shoulder of Thistle's dress. Suddenly something deep inside Fischer was triggered, a distant but nagging memory. He focused on Thistle, trying to understand what it was about her that was so familiar.

"He's going," David said. "It's decided. As soon as we work out the details, we're on our way. Right, Fish?"

Fischer remained silent. He felt as though whatever had happened that day had stood him squarely on a threshold. He had waited and watched as he always did, staring deeply into the black unknown, but now he felt her tugging at his arm, this strange girl, urging him to step over to the side of uncertainty.

Then recognition hit him broadside as he dared meet her gaze head-on. This Thistle—she was the pale girl in blue from his dreams.

Fischer glanced from David's hard-set face to Thistle's expectant one. He could barely speak, yet he knew they were waiting for his answer. "That's right," he said. "We're going."

Even David looked a little surprised. "There's a lot to

be done. Right before the tremors started, I got the answer to our question."

He handed Fischer the printed copy of his computer search.

```
What is the exact center of the
United States?

GeoWiz: After Alaska and Hawaii
joined the Union, the geographical
center became a point slightly
west of Castle Rock, South
Dakota.
```

Fischer stared at the paper. "South Dakota? You've got to be kidding. That might as well be a million miles away."

"You witness the genesis of the world's end." Thistle looked up at them. "We must reach this faraway place before three nights have passed. Then my father will travel on, and my protection as Keeper will end. But is it possible to reach this place so quickly?"

"Everything's possible." David smiled and jumped to his feet. "We just have to figure out how."

"Let's get you some clothes," David was saying. "You're gorgeous in the dress, but denim travels better, believe me."

Thistle laughed. Fischer wondered if she even knew why. But he did: She was caught in David's spell.

"I have some old jeans and shirts that might fit you." David offered Thistle a hand to pull her up. "There's a lot to be done. We'll need maps, food, sleeping bags, a camp stove. Lucky for us, we're already supposed to be gone this weekend, so no one will suspect. Remember, Fish? The woods? Camping?"

"Yeah, I remember," he said, but the truth was, he'd forgotten almost everything that had happened before Thistle had arrived.

As he stared out the windows, Fischer had a terrible feeling that they were headed someplace far wilder than the Georgia woods, someplace as unknown and foreign as the surface of that moon.

/ / /

Atlanta Noonday News

Channel 5

July 12

Brent Lanier: *Today, earthquakes registering six on the Richter scale were felt in the area all the way from Atlanta to Asheville. In a region known more for its beautiful mountains and national forests, the tremors took many by surprise, but fortunately, though many were "shaken," few injuries were reported.*

Katie Wescher: *Oh, please. But seriously, Brent, no serious structural damage? I guess we should consider ourselves lucky.*

Brent Lanier: *Very lucky, Katie. The only exception seemed to be this employee parking deck in Atlanta. Let's see if we can get a close-up of that.*

Katie Wescher: *It appears to be nothing but rubble. But fortunately, because this building had lost power after this morning's heavy storms, many of the employees had been released to go home. Otherwise those decks would have been filled with cars.*

Brent Lanier: *Fortunate indeed. But the real news seems to be the weather, which went from heavenly to hellacious. Stay tuned for your revised forecast, but in case you haven't looked out your window lately, heavy precipitation has settled over the metro area, with no end in sight.*

/ / /

All things were made by him; and without him was not any thing made that was made. In him was life; and the life was the light of men. And the light shineth in darkness; and the darkness comprehended it not.

—*John 1:3–5*

CHAPTER SEVEN

As he stared through his windshield wipers at the garishly lit stretch of the city, the man in the dented white Corolla had his mind on the phone call he had received from his wife. His basement was flooded, two feet deep in water and gaining fast. He should have listened when his wife told him to put in that sump pump last spring. Now it would cost him a fortune to fix. A moment later he rounded a curve coming out off the connector and saw a man in a dark coat walking down the middle of the eight-lane highway. He swerved to miss him, but instead, the car hit the median wall, and his head slammed into the steering wheel, shattering his glasses before he passed out.

But the walking man did not look back at the accident or hurry to help the driver of the car. If he had smelled imminent death, so intoxicating, he would have stopped, however briefly. He would have proudly pressed his hat to his chest like a new father, seeing his son for the first time. Granted, there was a chance that the driver was not one of his own, but that seemed unlikely. Those seemed few and far between these days.

The rain became a deluge, but it did not faze him; in fact his skin repelled it as though it were the waterproof coat of a seal or a beaver. Each step he made on the slick ground became a dry, steaming place for the raindrops to fill again. The vast amount of water, the swaying trees, the lightning that scratched over the heavy surface of the darkness excited him. And why not? He had felt the change in atmosphere the moment the Stones were separated. He strode down the highway, ignoring the blare of horns that faded like gunshots as cars passed him and raced into the night.

His mind was on important matters. The Taker had arisen, as it had been predicted. But that was long ago and men had forgotten, just as they had forgotten the Stones, the relics their ancestors carried with them when at their exile from paradise. From that time forward he had attempted to possess the Stones, yet he never had. The Keepers had held them from him, but that was all about to change. His time had come, and rightly so. The tale had been passed down through the centuries. He had endured, most certainly, but how long these words had plagued him.

And it came to pass in the days of the ancients that the sky
darkened and gave up rain and ice and the earth did shake and
the mountains spewed forth their entrails. So the wise men and
the priests and the rabbis and the holy men held council. And it
was determined that the Stones, with their consummate power,
should be kept from the grip of Evil, so that the land and the
sky and the seas would be tolerable for life.

Belial stopped in his tracks in the middle of the highway. Now that the Taker had arisen, as he had lately heard
it said, the odds had swung back in his favor. But how to
find this Taker? Belial sniffed the sodden air. A boy. How
delicious.

Then almost at once, the scent was lost, for the Stones,
held so long by the Keepers, muddied his sight and senses.
Still, from time to time he caught a whiff of the scent
again, and then his hunger for the Taker, for the Stones,
was insatiable.

Lightning struck overhead, but Belial stopped only to
admire the sky. No matter, he thought. No matter that he
would have to rely on his people, his Own, to find the
Stones. They would be found, and when they were, he
would arrive on the scene, as he had so often dreamed, and
take possession.

And it is foretold that One will arise, an ordinary man, with
all the weaknesses of a human. And in separating the Stones

from the Keepers, he will become the Taker. And the skies will open as they did in ancient days, and the winds will run foul over the lands, and the earth will break like bread. And the world shall remain this way until the Taker's Stone is claimed by Light or Dark.

But as the Stones were created from portions of good and evil, so shall be the Taker's heart. Thus no man shall know the fate of the world until the Taker is tested. Then either Light or Dark will rise and prevail. Light or Dark will prevail. Light or Dark will prevail.

Belial smiled. Oh, my, yes, he would find the boy, this Taker. He stopped in the road and held his arms wide open as the rain drummed down more heavily. The boy was his ace in the hole. For who would not agree? Belial was nothing if not persuasive. He would gain possession of the Stones and put an end to the Keepers, and then oh, the infinite pleasure, the changes he would make to this miserable world.

He stroked his chin, and where his fingers raked over his skin, dark hair issued forth. He touched the place directly forward of his ears, and the same hair grew upon his head. Oh, yes, he was beautiful. He could be beautiful in every way imaginable. Irresistible truly, like the Stones themselves. He closed his eyes, and a car pulled over to the side of the highway.

The passenger window cracked open a little, and he

could see a woman in a business suit inside. "Have you had an accident? Can I call someone for you?" the woman asked, holding up a phone from the wood-paneled console beside her.

He smiled warmly, and the woman hung up the phone and unlocked the door. "Would you like a ride?"

"I most certainly would." The man hooked his index finger over the top of the open window. "You see, I relish the open air, but you have reminded me how imperative it is that I reach my destination in a timely manner. What's more, I've been meaning to have a little talk with you for some time."

He opened the door and let himself in. "You might fasten your seat belt, my dear." The door slammed shut. "I have a distinct feeling that we're in for quite a ride."

I Daniel was grieved in my spirit in the midst of my body, and the visions of my head troubled me. —Daniel 7:15

CHAPTER EIGHT

It was two twenty-seven on the afternoon of the earthquake when the news came. His mother had checked into the hospital with labor pains, and Aunt Kathy and Uncle Matthew were frantically packing to leave.

As Fischer and David were sweeping up the last of the plaster dust, Aunt Kathy appeared on the stairs.

"Fischer, your uncle Matt and I have talked it over. If you agree, we'll leave things as planned. You and David will go to James's for the weekend and we'll go to help your mother with the baby." She took another step downward. "We could come back for you on Monday when we have your mother settled in. What do you think?"

Fischer stared at Aunt Kathy's hand on the banister. "I don't know." He knew it was a stupid answer, but he was torn, annoyed by his indecision. "I wanted to be there. She'll be alone."

"She won't be alone, Fischer. Mom and Dad will be with her," David said.

Fischer could almost read David's thoughts. Why make waves? This was their chance to leave with Thistle.

"If you want to come with us, you can, of course. I wouldn't want you to be worried. David can still go to the Blacks', and you can drive to Leeland with us. Think about it, dear, and let me know." Aunt Kathy turned, then stopped. "But if you are going, you'll have to get packed right away."

Fischer watched her climb the stairs, knowing that David was only keeping his peace till she was out of sight. He barely waited till Aunt Kathy disappeared around the corner. "What's wrong with you? You heard Thistle. She has only three days. Now we're wasting part of the first one talking about whether to do this or that."

"Stay out of this, David. I have other people to consider."

"Oh, really? Who? Your father will be home in a couple of days, and in the meantime, my mom and dad will take care of your mother. Look." David stepped closer to Fischer. "She'll be okay, I know she will. But if we wait any longer, Thistle won't be. There isn't time for a dress rehearsal. I'm going to get ready. You do what you want."

As David disappeared down the hall, Fischer propped the broom against the wall and lowered himself onto the stairs, wishing for once he could be as sure about every-thing as David seemed to be.

He stared into the lamp hanging above him in the foyer, and his thoughts began to fragment. Outside lightning flashed. The lamp began a gentle sway, casting moving shadows on the wall that seemed like the beginnings of a dream.

In the glass globe of the swinging lamp, the light flick-ered off and on, and a picture appeared. The Shadowy Figure was there, vague and motionless. Fischer's breathing slowed as he stopped struggling with thoughts of what he should do and allowed himself to float as though he were a leaf carried by a stream. Now a light carried him for-ward, and he drifted into it, watching the picture build into muted shapes and lines.

The lines and shapes became a wide-lens view of forests and rivers and cities, and oceans and continents, and then the whole world appeared like a mottled ball before him, swaying slightly until it began to disintegrate.

Next, as though the view in the lens were being nar-rowed, he saw a vast stretch of land, the town of Leeland, a cluster of buildings. Suddenly he was inside a small room. His mother was there, dressed in a smock, smiling in that way of hers that always made Fischer smile, too. He knew the place where she lay was a hospital room. He rec-ognized an adjustable bed, a gray pitcher on the bedstand, a woman dressed in white who strapped a monitor around his mother's protruding belly.

All at once the hospital room became disjointed, and Fischer saw only snatches of images. His mother staring down with tears in her eyes. The baby in her arms. Suddenly he was there, a part of his own dream. His mother looked up, her face brightening with recognition. He held something out to her in his outstretched hand, or maybe he was only trying to reassure her. But now he saw the Stone resting in his palm, and the coldness in his face made him want to shut his eyes. His mother's smile faded to confusion as his fingers closed over the Stone and he turned toward the door. The images began to break up. "Put it back, Fischer," his mother begged. "Please." Then, above her, the roof began to cave in, a baby was crying, but over all the noise he heard the Fischer in his dreams say, "No, it's mine." There was a terrible scream, and a moment later he was left staring at the hanging lamp flickering in the storm and listening to Uncle Matthew's voice upstairs.

Fischer was on his feet at once, breathing as though he'd run for miles, his pulse throbbing under his skin. He wiped his hands down the sides of his jeans and tried to think clearly. Even if he didn't completely understand what he'd seen, he knew something was terribly wrong and that somehow, it had to do with his taking the Stone. What choice did he have now but to try to fix whatever it was he'd broken?

He staggered up the stairs to Aunt Kathy and Uncle Matthew's bedroom and knocked on the doorframe.

"Fischer?" Aunt Kathy looked up from her packing. "You're so pale. Are you sick?"

"No, I'm okay." Fischer eased into a chair. "It's just that I've thought about it, and you're right. I'll only be in the way back home. It would be better if I stayed here with David."

Aunt Kathy perched on the edge of the chair and observed him. "You're sure? Because if you're not, maybe Matt should go ahead and I should stay here."

"No, you can't," Fischer said. "Mom is counting on both of you. I'd feel worse if you didn't go."

Uncle Matthew threw a stack of shirts into a suitcase. "Kathy, I'll call the Blacks and tell them that we're leaving."

"David and I will call," Fischer told him, trying to sound helpful. "You just go."

Aunt Kathy gave Fischer a hug. "I promise we'll let you know as soon as you have a new brother or sister."

Fischer was suddenly panicked. A phone call from Aunt Kathy and Uncle Matt to the Blacks would blow their cover. "But we'll be gone. Camping, remember?" he said.

"Then call us in Leeland once you're back." Aunt Kathy smiled. "Sure you're okay?"

Fischer nodded. "Sure."

"I'll come back for you guys in a couple of days, when the hubbub is over, and your mom is feeling rested." Uncle

Matthew winked at Fischer. "I know you want to be there, but she'll be fine, Fischer, I just know it."

Fischer knew, too. Somewhere within the pictures he'd seen, his mother had held a baby in her arms. She'd been smiling, happy—until he'd appeared holding the Stone. Somehow he had to make sure that her happiness wasn't something that he'd destroyed.

"I'll tell David." Fischer left the room before the tightness in his throat gave away his fear.

He slipped down the basement stairs and opened the storage closet door slightly. Thistle was sitting bolt upright in the torn yellow chair David and Fischer had stashed in the closet just that morning. "It's time," Fischer said. "We'll come and get you when they've left."

Thistle rose to her feet, her blue eyes luminous. She suddenly looked very young in David's long-sleeved white shirt and a pair of Fischer's faded jeans and bulky socks. "Make haste. I shall be waiting."

As Fischer watched his aunt and uncle roll their suitcases down the slick sidewalk to their car, he waved to them from the front door, trying to appear lighthearted. Despite the slapping windshield wipers, Aunt Kathy held up the note Fischer had written to his mother, telling her he loved her, that he couldn't wait to meet his new brother or sister. As the car pulled away from the curb, a part of Fischer was relieved, while another part wished only that he were inside it.

When the car turned at the end of the street, Fischer called Thistle up from the basement, and David picked up the phone and began to dial.

"What are you doing?" Fischer asked.

David held up a finger. "Hello? Mrs. Black? My aunt's in labor. Right. Fischer's mom. We're headed out of town right now. Will you tell James we're sorry to have to cancel out?"

David smiled at Fischer. He had that look on his face that Fischer knew so well: David was back in the driver's seat. He didn't miss a beat as he tossed a glass paperweight from Uncle Matthew's collection in his hand, then put it back to take the last bite of his bagel.

Fischer's own stomach was growling. In the midst of all the confusion he'd forgotten to eat. For Thistle's sake, he should be glad David was the one who'd initiated this trek they were planning. If he had to pick between David and himself to save the world, even he would pick his cousin.

"It is a done duel," Thistle announced as Fischer and David joined her in the pantry.

"Done *deal*." David corrected her. But as she turned away, he reached out and touched Thistle's hair. The gesture was so quick that Fischer wondered if she'd even noticed. But *he* had.

Flashlights were loaded with new batteries, sleeping bags rolled in parkas, and a pocketknife, lighter, and map of South Dakota placed into a Ziploc bag and tucked away into the side of a backpack. At last David left Fischer and Thistle to check the house and lock the doors.

"It speaks well of you that you chose to come," Thistle said.

Fischer did not answer, pretending to be too intent upon loading his pack to hear her. He guessed that David had told her all about him, and none of it good. Knowing his cousin, he'd probably given Thistle a blow-by-blow account of all of Fischer's failings, but David couldn't say anything now—Fischer was going.

By three o'clock they had locked the door of the old yellow house behind them and were making their way through the woods, across the plank that forded the swollen stream where Fischer had fallen only the night before. The path they chose led them along a side street and into an alley in back of Aunt Kathy's travel agency office. David inserted a key into the back door and turned the doorknob.

"Who's there?" someone called. Fischer and Thistle dodged sideways as a woman in a rolling chair swung around from a cubicle wall. "Oh, hi, David," Fischer heard her say. "I'm the lucky one on call today. Fun, huh?"

David shrugged his shoulders apologetically. "I'll only be a minute. Mom asked me to pick something up."

"Okay, well, let me know if you need help."

David signaled Thistle and Fischer to follow him into an office down the hall, then closed the door behind them.

He booted up the computer on his mother's desk and typed in the security code he had taken from her file at home. "Keep an eye on Mrs. McLean, Fish. I need about five minutes to do this."

Through a gap in the slats of the blinds, Fischer saw the woman with coiffed auburn hair looking through papers at a wide desk.

"Next flight to Rapid City, South Dakota." David clicked his tongue while he waited for an answer. Then he groaned. "Not until tomorrow morning."

"No," Thistle insisted. "We cannot wait."

"How about cities close to Rapid City?" Fischer asked.

David typed on the keyboard and waited again. "Here's one. Not exactly the answer to our prayers, but we can connect in Salt Lake City and fly into Pierre, South Dakota."

Fischer pulled the map from his backpack and found Pierre west of Rapid City by a hundred or more miles. "If that's as close as we can get."

David's fingers tapped the keyboard. "Okay, we're on the afternoon flight, and we have a return day after tomorrow. Mom and Dad won't be home till the day after that."

"You're sure this whole thing will work, right, David?" Fischer asked.

David folded his hands behind his head while their tickets printed out. "Trust me."

Thistle shot Fischer a beaming smile, but he couldn't

share her enthusiasm. He'd seen too many of David's plans fall apart because he hadn't thought them through.

As they hurried toward the back door and slipped outside, Mrs. McLean waved good-bye, a single flapping hand over the top of the cubicle. In a moment they were dodging through the rain for the path in the woods again. At the crest of Hailey Hill Fischer stopped to look down on Aunt Kathy and Uncle Matt's house on the quiet street below. A moment later he turned back and saw that David and Thistle had stopped to wait. David motioned to him impatiently, but Thistle's hooded poncho hid her expression.

As Fischer forged on behind them, the sound of rain provided an excuse for the ensuing silence. What did the future hold? Fischer wondered. Would he ever see his mother again? Or know his new brother or sister?

Something had awakened inside him, something stirred by the images Fischer had seen earlier in the hallway. He was back on the threshold, only now he felt himself leaning over the edge, testing the limits of previous boundaries. He stored those thoughts away and hurried to catch up down the hill.

On the bus ride from the outskirts of White Horse to the airport in Atlanta, they hardly spoke, or looked up as they got off the bus and headed through the terminal.

When they reached their gate, they split up as agreed, and Fischer positioned himself in the line at the ticket counter. Despite his attempt at composure, his hands trembled as the ticket agent called him forward.

"Do you have identification?" the man asked.

"What kind?" Fischer asked. He hadn't expected the question. "I'm fourteen."

"But you're traveling alone?" the agent asked.

"No, I'm with my cousins," he said. "My dad dropped us off, and we checked in at the front counter."

The agent flipped through their tickets. "Your father should have checked you in himself."

"Oh, really? Well, he's already gone." Fischer's heart was pounding as he took out his student identification and handed it to the agent. "I showed this to the guy at the front counter, and he said we were okay."

"How much longer will this take?" the man behind Fischer asked.

The agent studied Fischer's ID. "You're old enough to travel alone, but in the future, have your father come in with you." He pressed some kind of stickers onto their boarding passes, handed them back to Fischer, then motioned to the man behind him to come forward.

As he left the counter, Fischer's palms were sweaty, but he focused on his sense of relief. Why hadn't David warned Fischer that the agent might question them? And where was David anyway? He spotted Thistle a few rows away. She looked so out of place among all the chattering passengers, with her hair stuffed under a cap, her serious expression, and her eyes focused on the 757 outside, that Fischer had to smile.

"Hey, how about this weather?" a kid in baggy jeans asked Fischer. "I sure hope it isn't raining where we're headed."

Fischer did not respond. The gate teemed with people. Business men and women sat guarding their briefcases and raincoats. Mothers led their children to the window to observe the baggage handlers dressed in bright yellow rain slickers on the tarmac below. Every phone along the walls had a waiting line.

Yesterday all of them would have seemed perfectly innocent to Fischer, but now he wondered. Was anyone watching them?

"Flight three-two-three to Salt Lake City is preboarding any passengers who need special assistance," the gate agent announced. "Any first-class passengers may also board at this time."

When Fischer and his mother traveled to museums in other cities, they'd established a routine: She took care of tickets; he took care of luggage. There was an element of trust involved. But this was different, nerve-racking— keeping tabs on Thistle and trying to locate David at the same time. If he didn't show up in the next few minutes, David would miss boarding, and Fischer and Thistle would have no choice but to leave him behind. Fischer jammed his hands into his pockets and began to rattle the handful of coins he had dumped there that morning. He remembered Thistle's warning: Every move the three of them made from now on was crucial.

Suddenly, from out of nowhere, his cousin appeared wearing a pair of sunglasses, newly purchased, pushed back on his head.

"Where have you been? We're practically ready to board."

"Peace." David stuffed his shirt into his denim shorts. "You worry too much. Everything's fine."

Two girls who stood near the telephones glanced in David's direction, then whispered and giggled.

"Passengers seated in rows ten through twenty, please board at this time."

Thistle looked up, and David nodded. She rose and shouldered her pack, Fischer followed, allowing a few passengers ahead of him before he filed into the single line that led to the plane. He absorbed the weighty sensation of heat inside the jetway, the voices of the men calling and laughing on the ramp below them. It all seemed so ordinary. But nothing was.

At last they entered the plane, and Fischer found his assigned row. He slid to the window and peered between the seats, trying to locate Thistle. Behind him David stuffed his backpack under the aisle seat, reclined his seat back, and pulled his baseball cap over his eyes. Thistle was two rows back, a man and a woman on either side. Still, Fischer did not breathe easily till the front door slammed and the plane moved away from the terminal.

He fell against his seat back, jostling the girl adjusting her headsets next to him. "Sorry," he told her.

"Folks, this is Captain Childs. The rain has things stacked up today. We're scheduled to sit on the runway awhile. Right now we have at least a dozen planes in front of us."

The girl gave Fischer a little shrug, and he heard the tinny sound of music from her Walkman as she closed her eyes. It seemed hours until the captain announced they were first in line for takeoff and the plane began to build up speed for the roll. Fischer leaned his head against the rain-streaked window and forced himself to watch the wilted grass beside the runway blur as the hum of the plane increased.

They were leaving, headed to South Dakota, a state as foreign as one of the countries in the books he liked to read. He was going to bring Thistle to her father.

The plane suddenly tilted up, and the ground dropped away. The shining pavement of the runway became low white clouds, a thick sweep of gray, and then miraculously, the plane rose to a place where pink and orange light shone on the egg crate surface of clouds below.

The drone of the engines made Fischer drowsy. He couldn't resist the sensation and closed his eyes. He saw him then, the Shadowy Figure, but the image was fuzzy, and he was too tired to try to bring it into focus. Then Grandpa appeared, clear as day, toasting him with a can of root beer. "Some things you have to trust, buddy," he told Fischer as he lifted the soda to his lips. For the first time in what seemed forever, Fischer slept.

/ / /

Air Traffic Control Tower
Pierre, South Dakota
July 12

Air Traffic Control: You have runway Bruno nine, US nine-two-eight.

Captain: Roger, tower.

ATC: Watch your approach from the south, US nine-two-eight; we had reports of wicked wind sheer from a plane that just landed, copy.

Captain: Appreciate that heads-up, tower. Visibility isn't great, either. Clouds are following us down, and the wind is brewing something nasty up here.

ATC: I don't like what I'm hearing, US nine-two-eight. Go around once, and come in from the north, runway Charlie two-six.

Captain: Will do, tower. I have a visual on that runway.

ATC: Come on down, US nine-two-eight. Can't seem to get the South Dakota weather to oblige today.

Captain: No problem, tower. We won't take it personally. The whole nation seems to be in the soup.

/ / /

O ye hypocrites, ye can discern the face of
the sky; but can ye not discern the signs of
the times? —Matthew 16:3

CHAPTER NINE

"So much for sunny South Dakota." David inspected the
gunmetal gray skies through the airport window.

A chill passed over Fischer as rain trickled down the
pane of glass, blurring the parked airplane outside.

"And it will soon grow worse," Thistle said.

"Let's head downstairs," David said. "Get ourselves on
the first bus out of this place."

Thistle nodded, then turned to Fischer. "Agreed?"

They turned away before he could reply. As Fischer followed them down the long hallway, he calculated that bus
fare would eat up most of the money they had collected
for the trip, sixty-eight dollars plus change. Still, the
sooner they found Solomon, the sooner he and David
could return to White Horse, and at long last he could go
home.

And what would home be like when he returned? It
seemed to Fischer, returning for the first time since

Grandpa had died, that it might seem only emptier, lonelier. Over the last years Fischer had spent more nights at Grandpa's house than at his own, especially when his mother was away at conferences or busy at the museum. It was Grandpa who insisted that Fischer attend school plays and games and, when he refused, took him to the movies and out to dinner. "Put a little zip in your life, would you, pal?" Grandpa had told him more than once. "You don't want to spend your whole life hanging around old geezers, do you?" Yet Grandpa never pushed too hard. He didn't make Fischer feel like a misfit—the way the kids at school sometimes did—for his interest in the museum or his history books, didn't make him feel like a strange specimen the way David had all summer.

"Fischer, the place where you live, is it like this one?" Thistle had asked that morning. They were in David's kitchen, packing for the trip.

"No." Fischer pictured the bungalow he shared with his mother, with its yellow walls and sparse furnishings and his room, which faced a backyard of overgrown privet hedge. "Our house is much smaller. It's just my mother and me. Well, till the baby."

"It used to be my greatest wish, to have a home," Thistle said. "But now anywhere I am with Solomon is home. For he is all that I have and all that I shall ever have." Fischer felt her watching him. "But I have not heard you speak of your own father."

It was familiar territory, this curiosity about Fischer's "missing" father. Fischer had covered the subject often enough, but how could he explain it?

"I don't see my father much," Fischer said. "He's always worked overseas."

"A pity. Duty is a heavy burden."

"Maybe," Fischer said. "But I can't see that it bothers him at all."

Thistle glanced up from her pack.

"Anyway"—Fischer avoided her eyes as he pushed his sleeping bag into its stuff sack—"he considers me a disappointment. He was hoping for someone a little more . . ." Like David, he almost said. "Well, let's just say I fall short of the mark. But it doesn't really matter. Our lives are separate now."

"You seem to have a keen sense of the past, Fischer. Then how can you not see that a share of your father's past and yours are one? He is a part of you, surely."

"Not the good part," Fischer said. He forced a smile. "Let's drop this, okay?" He was thankful that Thistle did.

Now, as they neared the terminal, Fischer couldn't help seeing the irony in the situation. At last he and his father had something in common. Fischer had left his own mother behind to help Thistle, a stranger by all accounts. As far as Fischer was concerned, his father did that very thing every time he left them.

All at once the sound of rain on the rooftop changed pitch, indicating a harder downpour. The throng of people who crowded the car rental counters and baggage carousels made Fischer stop and drop his pack.

"What is it?" he asked a woman seated amid a pile of suitcases. "Has something happened?"

"Well, young man, that depends on where you're going." The woman fanned herself with her newspaper. "You're okay if you're headed east, but if you're going west, you won't get to Rapid City tonight."

"Why not?" Fischer asked.

"Fellow renting cars tells me that so much rain has fallen in the last twelve hours, some of the roads have washed out. People can't get where they need to go."

"No sweat," David said. "I'll take care of this. There's got to be a way out."

Fischer started to tell David that not even his charm could change bad weather and washed-out roads, but his thoughts were interrupted when a man bumped into him.

"Sorry," the man said. He turned back to face a bedraggled-looking group of kids.

"Everyone here for Camp Prehistoric?"

The kids, rolling suitcases and sleeping bags, studied one another casually.

"Okay, here's the deal," the man said. "I'm responsible for getting you people to camp. We'll be splitting up into groups to travel—two by bus, one by van."

A kid raised his hand. Fischer recognized him from the airport in Atlanta. "How far is this camp anyway?"

"In Kadoka, a couple of hours away if the main roads are open. But because we've had some flooding, they very well might be closed. Then we'll have to find some other way around."

This announcement was met by groans, but Fischer's mind had stopped on the name Kadoka. He had rubbed his finger over the dot that marked it as they studied the route map spread on David's kitchen table. It was no more than an hour from Rapid City by car.

David pushed from the crowd. "Bad news. No more buses out tonight."

Thistle hoisted her bag. "Then we proceed on foot. We cannot afford to lose more time."

"If there aren't any more questions," the man with the group said, "we'll claim our luggage, get it loaded up, and go."

David picked up his pack and helped Thistle put on her pack. "You've got the map, Fischer. You'd better start figuring out fast how we'll get where we're going."

"Wait," Fischer said.

David looked up, annoyed, but Thistle looped her thumbs through her pack straps and observed Fischer.

"We're wasting time. What is it?" David asked.

"Those kids behind us are heading to camp," Fischer said.

"So?"

"The camp isn't far from Rapid City. I remember from the map," Fischer said. "What if we just pretend to be with them?"

David and Thistle stared at the group assembling to leave.

"Yes. It might work." The shine in Thistle's eyes made Fischer suddenly recall how beautiful she had looked standing in the blue dress. Only now, her expression was a mixture of surprise and curiosity. "It appears the journey has begun. Well done, Fischer."

David did not look as pleased.

"First ten people, right through those doors." The man with the clipboard didn't seem to notice as the three of them joined the group. He motioned with an exaggerated wave to a girl behind the wheel of the Camp Prehistoric van, then hurried back to the rest of the campers waiting inside the terminal.

While the others climbed into the van, Fischer lingered behind with Thistle and David. They boarded last, taking the seats closest to the door in the event a quick escape became necessary.

"What's wrong?" The driver pulled away from the curb as they were getting settled. She studied Fischer in the rearview mirror. "You look queasy. Turbulence coming in?"

Fischer nodded.

The girl made a face, pushed the mirror back into place, and flipped on the radio. "This weather's a bear," she grumbled.

As the van moved away from the airport, Fischer became almost numb with relief.

"More rain for central South Dakota," the radio announced. *"Hands down, the most unusual weather recorded in these parts for decades. Much as we usually appreciate a few rain showers this time of year, folks, this much is downright scary."*

Fischer could not tell if Thistle or David had heard. Their heads lolled on the seat backs as though they were sleeping. Fischer stared out the window and watched the city pass. VISIT THE BADLANDS, a billboard read.

He closed his own eyes to rest, and the Shadowy Figure from his dreams materialized. How did night dreams become daydreams? When he concentrated hard on the reappearing figure in his head, he recognized the tall, lithe frame of a man, but Fischer's head began to hammer with a numbing ache the moment he opened his eyes.

He wanted to ask Thistle about the man, but not now, not yet. If David heard, he would only twist his words around to make Fischer look ridiculous or crazy.

His mind flipped back to the images of destruction he'd glimpsed in the hallway lamp. Maybe those pictures had been there all along, but because he hadn't believed, he couldn't see them. His mother had once told him that Native Americans welcomed, even encouraged the opportunity to "know" things through visions. But instead of sharing that enthusiasm, Fischer was afraid. Once he saw, once he knew, would daylight or darkness ever be the same?

Enough, Fischer thought. Let me rest. Let it be enough to rest without knowing what it all means. The sound of the rain and the hum of the van's engine had made him sleepy.

He awoke with a start to the van bumping down a gravel road and the smell of pine and wet dirt. They passed a sign he could barely make out. CAMP PREHISTORIC. Darkness surrounded them in high, dense walls. Fischer checked his watch. Three hours had passed.

Though David and Thistle were asleep right beside him, Fischer felt suddenly alone. He slid to the edge of the seat to try to establish his bearings. The escaping light of day was sapphire over the blunt-featured crags of dark hills.

He was aware of the warmth of Thistle's skin near his own. She's counting on you. The words popped into his head, clear and perfect as the notes of a dog whistle, unheard but urgent. From what Thistle told him in White Horse, a lot more than just her life was riding on his getting her to Castle Rock in the next two days. But for now he had to be honest with himself. He was there because of his vision but also for Thistle. She was what fueled him beyond his own fears.

The first star of night appeared like a beacon, pale as Thistle's face. Something buoyed him up then. Something like hope. For better or worse, as Thistle said, the journey had begun.

For we wrestle not against flesh and blood, but against principalities, against powers, against the rulers of the darkness of this world, against spiritual wickedness in high places. —*Ephesians 6:12*

CHAPTER TEN

They waited while the van emptied outside Camp Prehistoric and the campers hauled their bags up the front stairs of a narrow barracks, stalling for time till the last person had disappeared through the building's double doors. When the van pulled away again, only Fischer, David, and Thistle stood under the dripping limbs of spruce trees next to the porch. But before they could even speak, a man's voice broke the silence. "Where do you think they've gotten to?"

The front doors swung open, and a wide chute of light fell over the parking lot.

"I thought Anna radioed she had dropped them off."

"She did," a woman's voice answered. "Called in fourteen, but we've checked in only eleven."

"They must have got by me somehow when I was in the men's." A scratching sound indicated fingernails against facial hair. "I'll just go check the hallway and see if they got lost."

"Yes, do that, Mr. Simonds," the woman said.

Thistle met Fischer's gaze as they listened to the man's feet retreating down the hall. The light from the open door shone long across the slick stones of the driveway to the front gates. Fischer shifted to see through a gap in the branches. The woman on the landing of the steps peered into the darkness, then descended the stairs, pulling her sweater closed against the night chill. At the sidewalk she scoured the landscape, ending her search in the direction of the woods, beyond the front garden where the three of them were hidden.

Fischer leaned away from David, curious to see the woman's face. The slant of her shoulders, the way she twisted her sweater buttons somehow reminded him of his mother, and that notion brought on a fresh wave of guilt, mixed with something stronger, something combining his desire to go back to the warmth and comfort of his old life with an irresistible curiosity about this new one. Fischer knelt forward as the woman turned toward him, then instantly fell back against David with an intake of breath.

David pushed him away. "What's your problem?"

But Fischer couldn't answer. The woman's eyes had become red pinpoints as she swiveled toward the noise. The man who had chased him across the fields last night. He'd had those same strange eyes, too.

Before she spotted him—and she would, Fischer thought, she surely would—the front door swung open once more, and white light washed out again, freezing her in time and place like a statue.

"Mrs. Goodlow? You out here?" the man called from the doorway.

The woman looked up, a picture of bland concern.

Fischer blinked hard. No glowing eyes or vampire teeth.

Now when he dared steal a glance at the woman, he noticed that her hair had begun to droop around her chin like limp curling ribbon. The skin around her eyes was smudged with lines and shadows, making her appear tired and worn out and very little like any kind of threat.

"Mrs. Goodlow?"

"Yes, I'm here, Mr. Simonds," the woman answered.

"I know those kids must be in the building, but I can't seem to locate them."

"Now don't you worry about that, Mr. Simonds." The woman's feet tapped up the stairs. "Wherever they are, I'll find them. Rest assured."

The door closed with a click, extinguishing the wide light, and the three of them darted around the side of the old building.

"It appears we have already been missed," Thistle said. "We must leave quickly."

"Fair enough," David said. "But the million-dollar question is, Which way do we go? We slept through the South Dakota tour coming in."

"I didn't sleep," Fischer said. "When we get to the end of the road, we head west."

"Fortunate that one of us was on the alert." Thistle nodded to Fischer. "Lead on."

"Three cheers for Fischer," David said.

Fischer shot a sidelong glance at David, who glared at him with icy irritation, but Fischer didn't care. For once he wasn't there just to act as a punching bag for David's overblown ego.

He darted away from the wall, hunched under the weight of his pack, and ran across the lawn wet from the rain, through the stone gateway, and onto the dirt road. The three of them had begun to slow from a run to a walk when two sets of headlights moved in their direction. From the shadows Fischer recognized the buses from the airport. Maybe the camp would be too busy checking in all those kids to search for them. At least for a little while.

As the lights of the camp fell farther behind and the night expanded around them, whirring sounds could be heard in the tall bromegrass along the roadside. Fischer's mind fell back to the woman's eyes and the eyes of the man in running shoes, red as the taillights of the idling buses. Why was he the only one who seemed to see them? He didn't really know what they meant, yet somehow he was sure it was trouble. Gut instinct, Grandpa would have called it.

"How do you know if something's bad, Grandpa?" Fischer had asked one night, years ago, as they sat on the sofa watching a ball game.

"Why do you ask me that, sport?"

Fischer hadn't wanted to tell Grandpa about the boy from the school bus who called him names and sometimes waited to grab Fischer's lunch and dump it into the trash can outside school.

"You're a smart kid, right?" Grandpa finally said.

Fischer didn't know how to answer that, so he lowered his head and said nothing.

"No, I'm telling you, Fischer, you're smarter than the average joe, so listen to me now. If you feel like something is bad, if you feel it right here"—Grandpa stuck a finger into his chest directly over his heart—"then most likely it is. Got it?"

"Sure," Fischer had said. Then Grandpa patted his hand, and it was over.

Now, in the darkness, David nudged his arm. "Wake up, Fischer. There's the highway. If you're going to play leader, better start acting like one."

Fischer looked up into the streetlights of an almost deserted strip of road. Any movement of cars or trucks was centered on a truck stop. The strains of a jukebox floated over the weedy ditch in front of the gas pumps and across the highway to where they stood.

"Looks like our lucky day," David said.

He motioned Thistle and Fischer across the road and past the pumps to the restaurant. The moment they opened the door, Fischer remembered that he had not eaten since morning. The odor of oil and diesel fuel was replaced by the smell of frying eggs and toast and hash browns.

"Is anyone else hungry?" he asked.

"Yes," Thistle said. "We might be wise to use this opportunity."

"My thoughts exactly." David smiled at her. "We'll order some food. Fish, why don't you take a look around this place? See what you can find out."

David gave Fischer an unmistakable nod. Clearly David wanted him out of the way so that he could be alone with Thistle, and Fischer knew better than to try to compete. What chance did he stand against David? He took a deep breath and wandered away from the counter and into the adjoining room.

The restaurant was crowded, with men mostly, drinking coffee and eating food that seemed more breakfast than dinner despite the fact that it was late at night. Fischer wandered between the tables as though he were in search of an empty one. He paused at the jukebox, hoping to overhear one of the drivers say that he was on his way to Rapid City, but instead, he only caught snippets of conversation about the rain and the flooding and washed-out roads. He turned back toward the front counter and almost bumped into a wiry man standing with his hands in his jeans pockets.

"Anything look good?"

Fischer shrugged, and the man smiled.

"This is one stinking night." The man held up two quarters. "You mind?"

"Go ahead," Fischer said. He began to walk away, but the man spoke again.

"When you travel as much as I do, it's the little things in life, you know?"

Fischer glanced toward David and Thistle, who were taking bags of food from the man behind the counter. "I guess."

"A measly song can be the one thing that keeps you going."

Fischer recalled his father's saying almost the same thing about the letters Fischer and his mother sent while he was away, though recently Fischer confined his correspondence to news about family and schoolwork. It seemed the older he got, the less he and his father had to talk about. He recalled his father's first day home this spring. Fischer had been in his room, studying some rock samples that his mother had brought home from a dig, when his father appeared at the door.

"There you are," his father said. "What are you up to?"

Fischer slipped the rocks into his desk drawer. The fact that Fischer seemed more interested in history than in the present or future was a sore point for his father.

"Nothing, really," Fischer said.

His father stood and looked around Fischer's room, his hands in the pockets of his khakis. "There's the football I sent you." His father went to Fischer's shelf and picked up the ball, then wiped a layer of dust from its surface. "Obviously you haven't used it much. I thought you were trying out for the team next fall. A team sport—"

"Builds teamwork." Fischer finished the sentence his father had repeated so often in his letters. Fischer wondered if his father would dare mention Fischer's football tryout last year, when he'd spent the better part of the afternoon being tackled and fumbling the ball and the rest of his time sitting out to ice his knee on the bench. "Face it, Dad," he said, "I'm never going to be a football star."

"I never asked you to be a star." His father gave Fischer an exasperated look. "But you can't experience much closed up in your room, Fischer. I'd hoped spending time with David might be a good influence on you in that regard. He's a confident kid. He has his share of swagger, admittedly, but the facts are, David seems to get where he wants to go." His father put the football back on the shelf and thumped it once. "The guy participates in life."

The skin of Fischer's face felt tight as stretched parchment. "Sorry," he said. He wished he could be around his father just once without feeling so small. "I have to get back to work. I've got homework to do." He turned back to his desk until he heard his father's footsteps move down the hallway and away from his room.

Now, in the bright light of the truck stop restaurant, the man at the jukebox jingled the change in his hand.

"Yeah, I've got a son about your age back home." The man dropped the coins into the jukebox and made his selection. "After a couple of weeks I can't wait to get back. He's hardly a kid anymore." The man looked reflective. "I just don't want to miss anything. Know what I mean?"

Fischer stole a glance at the man as "Tightrope" began to play.

"These must be friends of yours." The man nodded to David and Thistle, who walked in their direction.

"What's going on?" David asked.

"Hi, my name is Will," the man said. "I was just about to tell your buddy here that I'm headed back into this stinking weather. So if you don't mind joining me till I finish my coffee, you're welcome to the table."

Thistle shot Fischer a questioning look, but David

smiled. "Great," he said. "In fact, that would be perfect. Seems like we've been running all day."

"Running?" The man pulled out a chair at the table for Thistle. "What are you running for?"

"It's a long story," David said. He took a sandwich from the brown bag and began to eat.

The man sipped his coffee. "Long stories are usually the best kind. Anything worth telling?"

A tiny chill crawled up Fischer's neck. "No," he said flatly.

The man looked up, surprised, and Fischer saw a glint in his eyes. He was suddenly aware of "feeling bad" in the way Grandpa had described all those years ago.

"My friend only means that we are in a hurry," Thistle said, casting Fischer a meaningful look.

A faint smile played on the man's lips. Then he stood and sorted some change from his pocket onto the table.

"Headed out, Will?" a man across the room called.

"Yeah, east to Cheyenne. I got one delivery in Rapid City; then it's a straight shot south down I-eighty-five." He turned back to Thistle. "It's been my pleasure, miss." His eyes swept over David, then Fischer. "A pleasure meeting all of you, but I've got to get going myself."

Fischer watched the man walk over to the counter to pay his bill.

"That was our ride, Fischer," David said. "It was ours for the asking. And you blew it."

"Maybe. But why get friendly? We don't know him."

"Fischer is right, David," Thistle said. "We can't trust the man's intentions."

"No offense, Thistle," David said. "But so far we've lied to my parents, stolen tickets, and flown halfway across the country alone. It's a little late to start being cautious, but it's not too late to get that ride. The guy's still at the counter. I'm going to ask."

"Don't," Fischer said. "Really, David. Something isn't right."

David followed the man's movements as he pushed open the glass door of the restaurant and walked toward the parking lot. "You're overlooking something, Fischer. If you've forgotten, we have only two days, and it looks like we're about to get another deluge. Need I say more?" He threw his balled-up napkin onto the table.

Thistle reared back in her chair and studied something on the far wall. "Perhaps we should consider what David suggests." A smile crept across David's lips. "With so little time, I fear we have little choice but to take any means of travel."

"I knew you'd come around," David told her. "On the other hand, if you're waiting for Fischer to agree with you, don't bother. You'd be waiting for days."

Fischer shoved back his chair and stood quickly, but David had already turned to slam open the door and was running to overtake the man in the parking lot.

Thistle stood beside him. "I have driven a wedge between you two."

"No, it's not that," Fischer told her. "David and I never see eye to eye." He watched the truck driver point to the place past the gas pumps where trucks were lined up one after another. The mist had become heavy since they entered the restaurant, and now it began to fall as drizzle as Fischer and Thistle stepped outside. They walked toward the black rig where David stood, and the truck driver grinned as he glanced up and saw Fischer's expression.

"You should have told me you had somewhere you needed to go." The driver pulled open the back doors of his rig, revealing a space half filled with crates. "It's not much. But it's home if you want it. You can stretch out back here and get some sleep, and I'll give you a shout when we get to Rapid City."

Don't do it. Fischer studied the man's face.

"How long do you think it will take to get there?" David asked.

"Not long." The man slid a toothpick between his lips. "Couple of hours, tops. Hop in, and we'll get this show on the road."

Don't do it. Don't.

David boosted Thistle into the trailer.

"Coming or not?" David asked as the rain began to fall, gluing Fischer's shirt to his skin.

"It's dry inside the truck," the man said. "And we've got

tornado warnings all over the state. Do yourself a favor, kid. And me, too. I'm getting soaked."

Don't. Don't.

Fischer shut the voice out of his head and pulled himself in after them.

The man slid the doors together. When only a narrow crack remained between the two, Fischer glimpsed the man's face. His eyes were the same red points of light he had already seen twice in the last twenty-four hours. Panic tunneled through Fischer, but then the sound of the door being shut into place was followed by a rattling noise. The latch was chained.

/ / /

Blue Darter: *Breaker, breaker, this is Blue Darter, do any of you big rigs copy?*

Southpaw: *That's an affirmative, Blue Darter. This is Southpaw. What can I do you for?*

Blue Darter: *Where are you situated, Southpaw? I'm coming out of Sioux Falls, trying to receive a ten-thirteen for I-ninety west to Rapid City.*

Southpaw: *I can do that for you, Blue Darter, we got roads out at Chamberlain and Wasta. This rain just won't quit, whatcha say?*

Blue Darter: *Definatory. Smokeys everywhere. Blood boxes wailing near the main bridge. Bad pileup. We got some mean weather out there. Copy.*

Southpaw: *I'm landing rubber for the night. Catch some Zs. Tornadoes springing up like oil wells in Texas. Too much can go wrong on a night like this. Over.*

Blue Darter: *That's a big ten-four, Southpaw. See you on the flip-flop. Hats off for the ten-thirteen. Watch yourself now and ride easy. Over and out.*

/ / /

But if thine eye be evil, thy whole body shall be full of darkness.

—*Matthew 6:23*

CHAPTER ELEVEN

Fischer yanked the door handle again. When it didn't give, he turned toward the beam of David's flashlight. "Did you see that?"

"See what?" David said.

Thistle looked at Fischer curiously. Hadn't she seen the man's eyes, either? He sank to the ground as the engine of the rig moaned through a series of gearshifts. How could he explain what he had seen to David or Thistle when he didn't understand it himself? "He's locked the doors," he said.

"So?" David rose and shone the flashlight around the sides, revealing stacks of boxes and high narrow vents at the roof of the truck.

"He's locked us in, David. We're trapped."

"He's a truck driver, Fischer. Forget whatever else you've got in your head." David tested his weight on a row of crates, then stretched out with his pack under his head.

"And locked or not, riding in the back of this truck is a whole lot better than walking."

"But—"

Thistle caught Fischer's arm before he could say more. She frowned and nodded in a way he couldn't decipher. "Let him rest."

Fischer looked around. He was soaked through and cold. The inside of the truck smelled like something sweet and earthy, potatoes or corn, but he could think of little else except that he had known something was not right, and now, because he hadn't trusted his intuition, they all were in some kind of danger.

Thistle clicked off David's flashlight. Without it, only the flicker of lightning through the high slats of the trailer made her outline visible. In no time David's steady breathing could be heard over the engine's monotone.

Fischer scoured each side of the truck, searching for a way out, but it was no use. Even if he piled up the crates and reached the slats, they appeared to be covered with a heavy screen. He wouldn't even be able to hang something outside to try to signal for help.

"Fischer," Thistle called softly, "come sit here beside me."

"You don't understand." Fischer kicked at one of the crates. "We're locked in. And we have no idea where this truck is taking us. I can't just sit and do nothing."

"When we see more light through those openings,"

Thistle said, "we'll know that we're near a town of some sort, and then, I swear to you, I will be the first to help you. Perhaps together we can make enough noise so that someone might hear and release us. But for now, come. Join me."

She spoke with such authority that Fischer lowered himself to the floor.

"Know this," she said. "Belial does little evil himself. He relies on others, the marked ones, for that."

Fischer sat up and turned in Thistle's direction. "You saw the driver's eyes, didn't you?"

"My own ability to see such things was lost when I was separated from the Stones, but I am not blind. I can read your reactions. And it is those reactions that give me cause to believe that you have secret powers unconfessed."

"But I don't," Fischer objected.

Thistle hesitated. "Fischer, your cousin lies sleeping. You have no reason to cloak the truth. For the moment it is only your words and my ears. But even if you do not choose to speak, the truth is evident without words: You still possess the Stones."

"I don't have them." Fischer slapped a hand to his heart. "I swear I don't."

Thistle did not lower her gaze. "Yet you cannot argue that we are being hunted. Obviously Stones are believed loose in this world, and with me separated from my father, Belial and others will be searching for them."

"But I don't understand," Fischer said. "What do they want? The Stones I took last night are gone."

For a moment Thistle was silent. "Once again, Fischer, weigh the consequences of your words carefully. How many Stones did you take?"

"I took two," Fischer answered solemnly. "And used them both."

Thistle shook her head. "Then perhaps it is I that Belial seeks. To destroy before I am reunited with Solomon."

Fischer squeezed his eyes closed. The Shadowy Figure from his dreams, was he this man, this Belial? He felt the insistent nudge of fear. "There's something else you should know."

Thistle turned her face toward him.

"I have these flashes, these images in my head. Like having a name on the tip of your tongue, but not being able to remember. I see things, but I can't make any sense of it."

Thistle's forehead furrowed as she studied Fischer in silence. "You have never had visions before?"

"No," Fischer said. "I've had dreams. Before I met you, I saw you in one of them."

Thistle leaned toward him. "Why did you keep this from me?"

"I didn't think you'd believe me," Fischer said pointedly. "Like you don't seem to believe me when I tell you I don't have your Stones."

He saw the flicker of a smile on her face. "About these

matters, your visions, your dreams, you need only know that what you see is or might become true," she said at last. "It is a rare thing to have this sight."

"Then why do *I* have it?" Fischer asked.

"That I cannot say, and I confess I am intrigued myself. But I must make certain that you understand the two forces at work in this world, Fischer. We are made of portions of both Dark and Light, and we must decide which rules us. Darkness is as it sounds, the absolute absence of Light. But Light is like a beam of sunlight seen through a prism. The sight you describe is like the beauty of the colors projected. They do not come from within; you are but the prism. They come from a more powerful source."

Fischer suddenly had a memory of the crucifix that hung over the door in Grandpa's house. The figure seemed odd to Fischer, flat, with crudely painted features and long, thin hands. But once when Grandpa had seen Fischer studying it, he had explained that it was not meant to be lifelike and real. It was made to be seen *through*, like a window.

Suddenly, as though someone had dropped a box of nails from the sky, the rain hammered down on the metal roof of the truck.

"I feel it is best to keep these matters between us. Belial might seek to use David if he senses he has any knowledge of the Stones." Thistle hesitated. "And now, now that I know you have the gift of sight, promise me, Fischer, that if I should not reach my father, you will be the one who will go in my place and tell him what has happened."

"Of course you'll reach him." Fischer squirmed, not wanting to think otherwise.

Lightning flashed through the slats of the truck, and Fischer glimpsed Thistle's face, pale and strained. She glanced over to where David lay sleeping. "I ask it as a favor. You must swear that you will go in my place."

Fischer hesitated. "If I have to, I'll do it. But I know I won't."

"Good," Thistle said. "And do not worry for me, Fischer. Since I can remember, my future has been uncertain. What happens to the Stones is my greatest concern, for in the proper hands, they could well exist forever. Solomon and I will not," Thistle said.

"So you're satisfied to only be this person, this Keeper?" Fischer asked. "I don't believe it. You must have dreams, things you hope for yourself."

"I told you I once wished for a home," Thistle said. "But what I didn't say is that we had one when my mother was alive, though I was little more than a baby at the time. We lived in the mountains. I remember the smell of burning fires in winter and the sound of goats through an open window and a bed painted with flowers. But the house was destroyed along with my mother, and Solomon, fearing for my life, has since made certain that we are never anywhere for very long."

"But someone must help you," he said. "You must have allies somewhere, friends."

"Our friends are those in the ancient monasteries sworn to secrecy. But even the faces in those places are not the same when next we pass. Age overtakes everyone we know and everyone we shall know."

Thistle leaned closer so that Fischer sensed her warmth very near.

"Once, though, when Solomon was sleeping, I befriended a girl my age on a steam train. She played a song hidden inside a box and offered to teach me a game in which common men could become kings, but she was never able to, for Solomon awoke and was angered."

"Because he thought the girl might hurt you," Fischer said. "Like—"

Thistle finished his thought. "Yes, like my mother. We left the train at the next stop, and I was melancholy for days, believing I would never see the girl again. Many years later, by chance, I looked across another platform of another train, and there she was."

"Many years?" Fischer asked. "How? You and I are almost the same age."

"I appear somewhat younger than I am," Thistle said. "My mother and father were already centuries old when I was born in the spring of 1807."

Fischer was glad that the darkness hid his expression.

"Anyway, no matter that I had changed so little," Thistle went on. "The girl did not know me. But though she was old and withered, I knew her immediately, for her eyes were still innocent. Now when I think of her, I imagine that this is how real people must live, what they must live for. To have such friends."

Fischer thought he had felt loneliness, but not loneliness like Thistle must have known. If only he had it in his power to see that she was never lonely again. For a moment he let his hand rest next to hers, and then she brushed her hair over one shoulder and studied him.

"You have friends, family," Thistle said. "Could you do it, Fischer? Give up those things you love and desire for the sake of something greater?"

"I don't know," he said. "It's hard to even imagine."

"Yes, it is difficult," she told him. "You have no idea how fortunate you are to live as you do. With so much possibility and choice. Solomon and I will never have that." She twisted a ring on her finger. "I envy you."

Fischer thought all at once of his father. "I'm not sure I have that much to envy."

Thistle laughed, and the sound made Fischer smile. She should laugh more, he thought. Maybe she *was* centuries old, and why would he resist that idea if he believed the rest of her story? But really, she was like him, still a kid. Why did duty have to take priority over everything? "Tell me about your father. How did he become a Keeper?" he asked.

"He was appointed long ago," Thistle said. "Among the Stones are two that are plain white. One bears Solomon's image, and one bears the image of the Second Keeper, first my mother and then me. All Keepers know the day of their duty has come by the appearance of this scar." She rolled up the hem of her jeans and pulled down her sock and as the lightning flashed, Fischer glimpsed a scar that looked like a half heart on her ankle. "Solomon likes to say that when he first met my mother, it was her pure heart and her name, which means remembrance, that caused him to recognize her as the Second. But my father is a romantic. He would never believe that he knew simply because my mother's image was revealed on the white Stone."

Fischer thought of the names etched into the leather pouch that held the stones. Then suddenly he and Thistle were thrown forward, and Fischer found himself bracing against a crate for balance. The light through the slats threw long shadows on the wall beside them.

From behind came a loud thud followed by a scramble of feet. "What's going on?" David asked.

The roar of the truck became the sound of a final downshift, then a gentle whine and a rattling halt.

"Why have we stopped?" Thistle asked.

"I don't know." Fischer boosted himself to the top of a stack of crates. "But I can make out a lot of other cars."

"What's the problem up ahead?" Fischer's heart began to hammer against his chest at the sound of the truck driver's voice outside. "Is that a roadblock?"

Fischer looked down and caught a glimpse of Thistle's sober profile.

"River flooded and the road's out," another man answered. "Where you headed?"

"Cheyenne," the driver said.

"If you don't know an alternate, you might want to stop somewhere for the night. I just heard on the radio that a slew of tornadoes were sighted west of here."

"If we're getting out, we'd better do it now," Fischer said as he climbed down from the crates.

"Now wait a sec," David said. "Is anybody going to tell me what's going on?"

"There isn't time," Thistle shouted. She began to pound the sides of the truck with her fists.

"What in the heck was that?" the man's voice said. "Hey, what have you got in the back of that rig?"

"Nothing," the driver insisted.

"There's a stiff penalty for transporting illegals." Now the voice that spoke was terse. "You'd better get them out of your truck before you get busted. Looks like it might be too late. There's a state trooper coming this way now."

The driver cursed and muttered under his breath as he worked the key in the lock. Fischer could hear Thistle's and David's shallow breathing as they waited.

"Thistle, stay close," he whispered. The moment the doors came open, they leaped out. Knocking the driver to the ground, they scrambled to their feet and bolted into the South Dakota night.

And he causeth all, both small and great,
rich and poor, free and bond, to receive a
mark in their right hand . . .

—Revelation 13:16

CHAPTER TWELVE

The truck driver, Will Frawley, waited to put some distance between himself and the state troopers who had pulled him over. He looked at his watch. Already past eleven. He wouldn't make it to his dropoff in Cheyenne, but he could cover his tail at work by calling in a busted axle. He'd tell his wife the same story. She'd heard plenty of his yarns over the years, one more shouldn't bother her, but that was the least of his problems.

He pulled onto a dirt service road behind a rise of rocks at the roadside and killed his headlights, so that now he could only see the rain drumming against the windshield. Compared with the pressure in his chest, the pain in his head was almost tolerable. He was for certain in trouble, the likes of which he had never seen. Of course now he recalled the promise he'd made all those years ago. But so much time had passed since he made it that he had almost forgotten, could almost convince himself that none of it was real, except for the mark on his hand.

It had happened when he was thirteen. He'd run away for the third time and was nearing the end of his rope after only a month. He was out of money and flat out starving, contemplating the possibility of going back to his father's temper when he saw an old man park his car at the road and walk down the narrow path to the river with his fishing pole. Will had waited in the bushes till the man was absorbed in tying a hook to his line, and then he had pounced and slammed a rock over the man's head. He was desperate, planned to rob him. His mouth salivated at the thought of having a real meal to fill his wrung-out stomach.

When he stood up and studied the old man lying motionless in the tall grass, his heart had been beating jackrabbit fast. And that was when the Man had come. Just appeared out of nowhere. Will was fixing to turn tail and run for the highway when the Man placed a hand on his shoulder and studied the old man at his feet like a bird examining a seed. Then the Man had turned to Will while he slid a pair of gloves from his pocket and pulled them on finger by finger.

"It appears you've done this man mortal harm, Will Frawley," the Man had said.

Fear drove through Will like steel rods. The Man knew

his name. "I didn't mean to hurt him that bad. I just wanted his money."

The Man had sat down in his long coat and swiped at his dusty boots before fixing Will with his cola-colored eyes. "Well, what shall we do about this?"

"I don't know," Will said. Then he thought he might know after all. "I guess you'll turn me in." He considered using the rock a second time.

The Man had laughed then, revealing pointed eyeteeth. "Have no fear, Will. Your secret is safe with me. I find nothing more distasteful than talent wasted in prison, although admittedly some of my best men have found a home there. Still, they can't be of use to me locked away, now can they?"

Will shook his head.

"I believe I can be of some use to *you*, though, as you could be of use to me. I wonder if we might strike a bargain?"

"What kind?" Will had asked, for even at the age of thirteen he had been the butt of some terrible scams.

"I will see to this matter." He nodded to the sprawled figure at his feet. "And when I have need of you, I will call on you to be my ears and my eyes. But when I call on you, and you have my word that I will, I expect your actions to be swift and flawless. I ask only that you agree to that."

"Sounds simple," Will had said. Too simple, really. He

hoped the Man wasn't stringing him along, planning to turn on him later. "Then what?"

"Then we will shake on it, and you will be forever in my care."

Will stretched his hand out and took the Man's. There was a sting in his palm that felt like fire, and he yanked his hand away with a curse. When he held his hand up, he saw a fresh burn in the shape of a coin. "What'dya do that for?"

The Man waved the question away. "A mere formality."

Then Will remembered the fisherman with blood seeping from the wound in his head and knew that either way he had gotten himself in deep. That had been more than forty years ago, and Will had almost forgotten, almost figured the Man was gone for good, but as soon as he had seen those kids at the truck stop, he'd heard the voice and known otherwise.

"Will." The word was whispered inside his head. "It's time. Be my ears and my eyes."

Will had looked around the restaurant and known that it was those three kids who had just blown in out of nowhere that the Man meant. He studied the kid standing at the jukebox. Lanky, wet hair, hands in his pockets.

"Bring him with you, Will," the voice said.

Will couldn't help it. The question just popped in his mind. "Why?"

Instantly he felt as though a band had been strapped

around his head. It pounded so hard he thought he would pass out.

"One of them has something I need, something we all need," the voice said. "But I cannot see to find them myself. That is because of their trickery. One of them carries a Stone."

Will was confused. What did a stone have to do with anything?

"But you can see the children clearly, can't you, Will? No need for questions, I only require you to be my ears and eyes. When you have secured them, you have only to picture where you are and I will come to you. You will do as I say, and I shall take care of this matter."

Suddenly Will had a flash of the old man lying at the riverbank, the man he had killed all those years ago.

Then he had done what the Man had told him, gone over to the jukebox and talked to the boy, but the kid had resisted. It was the other one who had run out after him. So maybe he had misunderstood, gotten the wrong kid, but what did it matter? The Man had said he wanted all three, and by some miracle, he'd had all three locked in the back of his rig till fifteen minutes ago.

A branch flew out of somewhere and hit the windshield of Will's truck, startling him into action. He pulled a ragged road map from under his seat with shaking hands and looked it over. There only one town close by, Dothan, and the way this weather looked, those kids couldn't get far. He would search until he found them, even if it took him all night.

He looked at himself in the rearview mirror. He didn't look so good. He wondered if it had anything to do with the pain in his chest like a vise being tightened between his ribs. The engine turned over with a rumble as he flipped the key in the ignition. He had to find those kids, no doubt about it. He didn't want to think about what would happen if he didn't.

/ / /

The Reliance Times

Reliance, South Dakota

July 13

MISSOURI FLOODS RELIANCE AS STORMS ROCK SOUTH DAKOTA

The heaviest storms in the history of South Dakota sent the Missouri River over its banks, buffeting the town of Reliance with a deluge of water. Pictured below is Selma Clinkston, holding a copy of the "Farmer's Almanac" page for the region, which she fished from the murky waters while waiting for local police to rescue her and her three cats from her rooftop. "I was sure happy to have something to read while I was up there," Mrs. Clinkston said of the almanac. When asked about what the almanac predicted for South Dakota's region 4 in July, she said, "Well, it said that everything would be normal, precipitation and temperatures both, but what's normal about all this?" Shortly after this picture was taken, Mrs. Clinkston and her three cats were rescued by boat and taken back to town, where she vowed to aid the Red Cross in its efforts to feed her stranded neighbors and their pets. "Times like these, you have to stick together," Mrs. Clinkston said. This may be good advice since it appears that there is no sign of the severe weather letting up today.

/ / /

For God speaketh once, yea twice, yet man perceiveth it not. In a dream, in a vision of the night, when deep sleep falleth upon men, in slumberings. . . .

—*Job 33:14–15*

CHAPTER THIRTEEN

As they stumbled into the darkness, the wind lashed Fischer's face. Each step sent them ankle-deep in mud or slipping across rock exposed by the downpour. By the time they found a narrow road, double ruts of water with weeds high through the middle, the night had grown soundless and still as the air inside a cavern.

"I don't like this," Fischer said. "It's too quiet. The air feels strange."

David raised his face to the rain. "We should have just stayed in the truck."

"That would have been an even bigger mistake," Fischer said.

"Look, Fish Head, just because you've convinced yourself that the truck driver was some kind of monster doesn't mean anyone else believes it. We asked him for the ride, remember?"

"You asked for the ride," Fischer said. "I didn't like the guy to begin with."

"Enough!" Thistle stepped between them. "Do you two mean to drive me mad? Surely you did not think we would traipse along, never meeting an obstacle?" In the distance a radiance broke through the blackness. "Look ahead. We must focus on our task."

"I'm too tired to focus on anything," David grumbled.

Thistle glanced from David's face to Fischer's, and though he pulled himself up a little straighter and tried to appear alert, he knew he must look as exhausted as he felt.

"Possibly a town lies ahead," she said. "I think we should move in that direction and seek a place of rest, at least for a while."

Fischer and David fell quiet as they followed Thistle into the town, which amounted to little more than a strip of small shops with a tapering of frame houses on either side. The wind began to blow again with a soft, moaning sound, sweeping a fresh fall of rain into their faces and whipping a torn canvas awning that overhung the street. Thunder rattled the glass of the storefronts.

On the steps of a dimly lit shop, Fischer stooped near the front windows and looked inside. He hoped maybe the place was empty, even contemplated breaking the glass just to be dry and warm for a few hours, but he stepped back suddenly, startled, as a face peered back at him through the pane. A moment later the door opened.

A man dressed in a faded shirt and overalls stood in the doorway. "What do you want? What are you kids doing out on a night like this?"

A brief silence was filled by the wind and a downpour of raindrops from the branches of a limp tree onto a van parked at the curb.

"I guess you've heard the roads are washed out," Fischer said.

"Have I heard? I was out in this mess earlier." The man broke into a smile, and Fischer felt they had passed some kind of test. "Well, you can't stay out in this weather, that's for sure. These kinds of storms turn into twisters. I'd let you use a phone, but the line went out about an hour ago. You'll have to hole up with the rest of us till the worst of this blows through."

The man ushered them into a small grocery store. At least it looked like one with its shelves of canned and packaged goods lining the front space, but a dog slept in a rocking chair by the checkout counter, a rug lay on the floor, and Fischer could hear laughter and voices from somewhere in the back. He was already beginning to feel more at ease when the door suddenly flung open wide and rain and leaves blasted in. The man in overalls fought it closed and bolted it with a turn of a key. "Lyddy!" he called. "We've got company."

A woman appeared from the back rooms. "I can see that." For a split second she looked suspicious, but then she asked, "How about something to eat?"

"Just something to drink if it's okay," Fischer said.

"Come on." The woman turned unceremoniously, leaving them to follow her to the back of the store, where the small room opened into another larger one.

A nest of kids in pajamas and twisted sheets were asleep on a pullout sofa, a stack of books and games scattered on the floor around them. Two women sat on a smaller sofa, speaking so intently that their eyes only flickered over Fischer when he entered the room. In a small kitchenette at the far end of the space some men played cards at a Formica table.

"More storm riders, Lyddy?" the oldest of the men asked.

"So it seems," the woman said. She took three sodas from a refrigerator and gave them to Thistle. "Help yourself if you want more. I'll bring you some towels."

The men at the table observed them with interest.

"We got washed out down the road," David volunteered.

"Yep." The second man, who wore his plaid shirt buttoned high, raised his eyebrows. "Hey, you don't play poker, do you?"

"You kidding me?" David smiled. "Five-card stud, draw, whatever."

"Hey, since it looks like you might be here for a

while"—the man raised his eyes as the wind scraped something along the rooftop, then leaned toward David—"care to play a few hands?"

"Why not?" David pulled out a chair and sat down as the man in overalls joined them at the table. Fischer watched at Thistle's side as David dealt cards all around.

"Now this"—over his shoulder David offered Thistle a glimpse of his cards—"is a perfect hand."

"Ah, you're bluffing," the man in overalls said.

"Ante up and find out." The man dissolved into laughter, and David caught Fischer's eye and shot him a wry smile.

That was the thing about David that Fischer admired: his talk, the gestures he had once tried to emulate before he understood that being himself really meant that he would never be David. He folded his arms and smiled back, grateful for the reprieve from his cousin's earlier mood.

As the cardplayers became louder and more animated, Fischer slipped back into the darkened part of the shop. He sank to the floor beside a radio that he had spotted earlier and tried to find a weather update. The radio emitted only continuous static. From the front window he could just make out a name on the post office wall across the street. Dothan. He checked his map. Just east of Rapid City, no more than thirty miles away. Satisfied that they could easily reach Castle Rock by the next night, he folded the map away and rested his head against the wall.

His eyes were heavy, but as soon as they closed, the dark figure emerged. Fischer blinked his eyes open again, determined not to see the man or anything more. As he turned his head and focused on the sleeping children in the corner, he recalled his own mother, his home far away. But his thoughts drifted back to Thistle.

He watched her across the room. She sat on a stool, smiling at David, who seemed to flush with the pleasure of her attention as he told his tall tales to the men at the table. Fischer suddenly felt so relaxed that he could almost believe that outside the sky was bright and clear. No rivers had flooded to wash out roads. No Stone had been stolen, and no lives unhinged because of it.

Despite his resistance, Fischer grew drowsy. His eyes closed, and he dreamed. He was running. It was night, and the rain fell in stinging waves. Something wailed behind him like a wounded beast, and Fischer tried to escape its grasp. The light from the creature's eyes flooded over him, and the sound it made became more guttural. But when Fischer turned to look into its face, he saw that the protruding yellow eyes did not belong to a living thing. Instead, they were the lifeless headlights of the truck driver's rig.

Then, all at once, the truck was gone. The sky was starlit, and he was racing through a field, a familiar meadow with a full moon overhead. Fischer sensed someone behind him once more and turned. This time it was a man who chased him, the man in running shoes from the campfire. Fischer raced into the woods and a moment later was huddled inside the thicket of the woods near the spring, just as he had the night he had taken the Stones. "You've got something, don't you, boy?" the man said.

But instead of crouching lower as he had that night, Fischer rose and faced the man's red eyes. "Yes," he said. Fischer opened his hand, and a glowing Stone lay in his palm.

"You know what you must do with it, don't you?" the man asked. Then Fischer saw the man's face change into the outline of the Shadowy Figure, and fear pierced his heart like a blade.

"Fischer?"

He jerked away from the hand on his shoulder, but his eyes snapped open, and he found himself staring into Thistle's face. He recognized the musty sweetness of the room and the laughter of the men playing cards. It was all right. They were safe. It had only been a dream. But there was something about his dream he wished he could remember.

"I must have fallen asleep," he said.

Thistle stooped beside him. "Yes, but a fitful sleep. What is it?"

"Nothing." Fischer pulled himself up. "Aren't you tired? You've hardly rested since we left White Horse."

"How can I?" Thistle sat down beside him. "There is too much to think about. It isn't the travel, of course—that I am used to—but being without Solomon seems so strange."

"It can't take us much longer to get to Castle Rock," Fischer said. "We're practically there now."

"Still, it will not be soon enough," Thistle said. "It is true what I said in the truck: I might not see the end of this journey. But if I do, and my father is not at Castle Rock, at the end of two more nights his protection as Keeper will cease, and Belial will surely have him killed. Have your visions revealed anything of the kind?"

"No," he said. But he suddenly realized that his visions might hold information that could help Thistle or hurt her. If she still questioned his loyalties, perhaps she thought he was keeping information from her now.

"Solomon and I have spoken of the possibility of his death once or twice," Thistle said. "But since he was the First of the Keepers and is wiser by far, I expected that I might be a more likely target for Belial. We have been together so long, just the two of us, that if another was to take Solomon's place—"

She lowered her eyes, and Fischer suddenly felt as inadequate as ever in trying to find the right words. He had done this: separated the Stones, taken Thistle from her father. No wonder she didn't trust him. He had no right to advise her, yet he felt he must say something. "We'll find Solomon, you'll go on, and David and I will head home as though none of this ever happened."

"Ah, that is what is called wishful thinking," Thistle said, pushing back her shirtsleeves, and tying back her hair. "The words of someone who has seen but one lifetime."

"Maybe. But it hasn't taken me long to figure out that you're strong and plenty smart." Fischer pretended to be watching the game across the room. "So even if you didn't have Solomon, you would go on. You'd protect the Stones. You said it yourself, you'll always be a Keeper."

"Yes," she said, "truly." But when Fischer stole a look at her, he could tell the subject was far from closed in her own mind. As usual, he felt useless and immobile, stuck for just the right thing to say that would bring her comfort.

He offered Thistle one of his balled-up sweatshirts to use as a pillow and crept into the other room. He passed the women asleep beside their children, picked up a game from the assortment on the floor, and took it back to where Thistle waited. She blinked her eyes open, and Fischer stood perfectly still, hoping that a miracle would occur and that the right words would come. When he opened his mouth to speak, maybe they would spill out the way they had the night he'd taken the Stones and called her name. It might be the only way he would ever be able to tell her what he felt, what he had known since he had recognized her from his dream. He should be the one she should be with. That was what he wanted to say in some perfect way that would make her believe in him completely.

"I know a game," he said.

Thistle's eyes filled with tears, though she blinked them away.

"In which common men become kings." Fischer sat down and opened the checkerboard between them.

Thistle cast him a smile that made him think that maybe, just maybe, even though she'd known him for only a day, she might have begun to trust that he would never do anything to hurt her. "I would like to learn such a game," Thistle said.

Fischer smiled in return, then opened the board to set up the players.

The time passed quickly. The wind howled overhead, and the branches cast shadows against the windowpanes and scraped the glass, but when the gray gloom of dawn broke on the horizon, Fischer heard the sound from his dream, the faint whine of an engine coming at a breakneck pace down the deserted road into town.

"Hey," Fischer heard one of the cardplayers yell, "what's that?"

Fischer felt the calm he had felt in the last hours evaporate as he ran toward the front of the store. There was the sound of chairs scraping the floor, and a moment later David appeared at the window.

"What is it?" the man in overalls shouted.

"I don't know," Fischer said. He was suddenly aware of someone at his side—Thistle—and of David only steps away, watching the two of them.

"I thought you'd be too absorbed in your *game* to notice anything else," David said.

"I'll tell you what it sounds like to me." The man in the plaid shirt glanced at Fischer, puzzled. "Sounds like somebody is in one heck of a rush to get here."

Then Fischer knew what he would see next. The twin beams of headlights as a truck barreled down the road toward them. "It's the truck driver," he whispered.

"What's that crazy fool up to?" the man in overalls said. "These roads are too slick for that kind of speed. Hey!" His expression changed to one of surprise. "He's headed right for us."

"Run!" someone in the back of the room screamed.

The man in the plaid shirt stumbled back in horror.

The truck swerved toward the steps of the shop, clipping the porch as it tried to brake, then fishtailed out of control with a sickening slosh of mud and gravel. It turned once, like a spun toy, and slammed into the building next door with a crush of concrete and metal and a burst of fire. The men from the card game pushed past Fischer and David and ran toward the cab of the truck.

Fischer turned and saw Thistle huddled far from the glass. He expected to see the same look on her face that he saw on David's—fear, panic—but he saw only sadness. "It's time," she said.

Fischer pulled David by the arm, and they scrambled away. They grabbed their backpacks, slipped by a woman jostling her crying baby, by the barking dog and the children, who held tight to their mothers' legs. As he hurried out the back door behind Thistle and David, he wondered, Was he running now as a fugitive might, away from the force that sought them? Or was he only fooling himself, or worse, being fooled, and stumbling headlong toward whatever patiently awaited them?

And if a house be divided against itself,
that house cannot stand.   —Mark 3:25

CHAPTER FOURTEEN

Fischer opened his eyes. Now where am I? He was lying on a floor of dirt, surrounded by a blinding glow. He recalled fleeing through the wet night air for what seemed like hours, the way becoming so rough and treacherous that at last they had taken refuge in what had seemed to be a cave. Then his dream from last night came rushing back.

He and his father were at the circus, just like the one his father had taken him to on his last visit home. Fischer remembered how angry he had been as he sat in the stands, angry that his father had picked the circus to begin with and not a place where someone Fischer's age would rather go.

But in his dream one particular clown stared in their direction, and as he caught Fischer's eye, he reached into his baggy pocket and took out a long handkerchief. His father was watching closely, thoroughly engrossed, but when the clown ran the handkerchief through his gloved hand and opened it, a blood red Stone rested in the center of his palm. Fischer jumped to his feet, searching the stands frantically for Thistle, certain she was in danger. He turned back in a panic, and the clown winked and clenched his hand, then unfolded his fingers again. The Stone had disappeared, and so had his father.

Now, as Fischer's eyes focused in the daylight, he distinctly smelled sulfur and dank rock. He felt a fine powder of dirt as he rubbed his thumb against the side of his index finger. Beside him Thistle was curled into a dirty and rumpled ball, and David was sitting near the opening of the rock, half hidden in shadow.

"You should take a look at this," David said.

Fischer stood and stared out into dim sunlight. As far as he could see, ripples of colored rock extended into ravines, and low hills rose suddenly into jagged formations. Though the day had seemed bright when he awoke, now clouds encroached in furrows, and a purple sky spread an ominous glow over the moonlike terrain. In that light the protruding rocks were transformed, as though at any moment they might begin to breathe, to split open and reveal grotesque contents.

"Where are we?" Fischer asked.

David tapped the map spread open at his feet. "It's called the Badlands," he said. "Care to guess why?"

With those words, the events of the previous night became real again. Fischer stood quickly and dusted off his hands. "We'd better get started."

"That's it? That's all you have to say?" David struggled to his feet. "You know, I don't get you, Fischer. This isn't pretend anymore. It isn't one of our games."

"It never was for me," Fischer said. "You knew that when we left White Horse."

"Well, I didn't think it would be like this."

"And if you did, would you have come?"

David crossed his arms over his chest. "Probably not."

Fischer hesitated, unsure how to handle this David. It seemed they had somehow traded places, and now Fischer had to find a way to make David go on. "Go ahead," he said. "Whatever is bothering you, just say it."

"You don't think she cares about you, do you?" David asked. "You understand, don't you, that she's only making you think she does so you'll help her."

Fischer didn't answer. It was David who didn't understand. He wasn't like Fischer, who had always felt apart. Now, at least for a little while, Fischer had someone on his side, someone who knew what being alone was like.

"You want to know what's bothering me, well, here it is. I don't like the way this whole thing is going. That truck driver from last night, I think you were right, he was after us. And if he was, how many others are? And why?" David cast a glance in Thistle's direction, and Fischer suddenly understood. David blamed Thistle.

"She doesn't like this any more than you do," Fischer said.

"Really?" David's face was taut. "Then by all means fill me in because that's not how I see it. I see us getting in way over our heads on her account."

Again Fischer said nothing.

"If there are things you haven't told me, Fischer, things I should know about her, about anything"—he squinted at Fischer—"then you'd better tell me now."

"Look, you're tired," Fischer said, trying to avoid David's eyes. There was so much that David didn't know, even if Fischer decided to tell him everything, where would he begin? Anyway, would Thistle want David knowing what Fischer did about her? "We've come a long way, David. As soon as we get to Castle Rock, this will be over."

But even as he said them, those words seemed false. Overnight his memories of life in Leeland seemed as distant and old as the artifacts in his mother's museum. What seemed real was this time, right now with Thistle.

David charged farther out into the strange sunlight. "I swear, I'm starved. I never thought I would miss my mother's cooking this much."

"Or a hot shower," Fischer said, trying to lighten the moment.

David looked into the distance. "Or my own bed."

This was something unique, Fischer thought, David needing something from him. And his cousin did need something, some kind of support that Fischer wasn't used to giving, an idea that made him feel uncomfortable and pleased at the same time.

"Listen, about home," Fischer said. "When we get into town, we should find a phone and call. We wouldn't want your mom and dad to call the Blacks first and find out we're not there."

Thistle ducked outside, squinting in the light. "Have I slept so long? The day is half passed." She fell silent as she took in the view.

"The Badlands," Fischer told her. "One of the geological wonders of the world, but also a national park. Which means there must be a road nearby."

"I can see one from this ridge," David called. "We've wasted enough time. Let's break camp and get out of here." He made a great show of folding the map and handing it over to Fischer, but Fischer could see that he was still upset. Did he still believe that their problems were all Thistle's doing, or was there more to it than that?

Thistle, busy with her own pack, did not seem to notice David's aloofness. As they headed off the ridge toward the road, Fischer had the sinking feeling that it would take very little to send David deeper into his present dark mood, something he would prefer to avoid at all costs.

As the afternoon wore on, the clouds Fischer had seen that morning became more brooding. They were fortunate enough to hitch a ride from a farmer within minutes of reaching the two-lane road. Fischer's spirits lifted at the sight of the beat-up yellow pickup truck veering off the highway and onto the dusty shoulder; maybe this was a lucky sign. As the three of them climbed into the back of the truck, the farmer rolled down his window and hung his head outside.

"Might rain," he said. "There's a tarp back there if you need cover. Got room for one inside."

"I'll go." David headed for the passenger's side of the cab without a backward glance.

"Have you and David fought again? He's suddenly quiet." Thistle climbed into the back of the truck.

Fischer propped his backpack in a corner. "He didn't sleep well, I guess."

They settled themselves against the sides of the truck and stretched out their legs. The pickup rumbled back onto the highway, and within minutes the wind was blowing past them in a way that made words impossible. Thistle smiled at Fischer, and he smiled back as she lifted her face to the sky. He watched the passing landscape of green grassland, trying to enjoy the ride. No point in worrying about David now. He could see the back of David's head though the rear window of the cab, but he couldn't read his mind, or change it for that matter.

By four o'clock the land beside the highway had changed from prairie to urban sprawl, and the farmer pulled into a gas station in Rapid City.

"Your friend's been talking in his sleep," the man said as he slammed the door of the truck. "He must be worn out."

"We've been camping," Fischer told the man. "His tent leaked, and he got drenched last night."

"So that's what the three of you have been up to, huh?" the man asked. "Camping."

Fischer sized up the man as he opened the gas tank of the truck. The man's eyes drifted in Thistle's direction. He was curious all right. Time to make tracks.

"Appreciate the ride, mister," Fischer said. "I'll call my dad to come and get us from here," he said, nodding to a pay phone. "We only live a few minutes away."

"I don't mind taking you," the man offered.

"Hey," Fischer called to Thistle, "wake David up and tell him we're there." He smiled at the man. "Thanks, but if my father finds out we hitchhiked back, we'll be in trouble."

"Can't blame him for that," the farmer called. "You can't tell who to trust anymore."

David climbed out of the truck with his pack. Fischer

motioned him and Thistle toward the pay phone in front of the gas station and waved good-bye as the farmer sped away.

"Oh, please," David said. "Do I smell food? Let it be real."

He pushed open the doors of the gas station and Fischer and Thistle exchanged a glance. David would be all right after all, Fischer thought.

"You go ahead," Fischer told Thistle. "I'm going to make a phone call."

Thistle followed David inside the store while Fischer dropped some change from his pocket into a pay phone outside and dialed his house in Leeland.

He waited while the number rang once, twice, three times. He'd been steeling himself, thinking he would actually have to talk to someone, but as the phone rang again, he realized that it was more likely that Aunt Kathy and Uncle Matt would be at the hospital and the answering machine would pick up instead.

He heard a click and then his mother spoke. "Hope and Fischer can't come to the phone at the moment, but please leave a message after the beep and we'll call you back." Fischer felt a pang at the sound of his mother's voice. He took a deep breath, trying to sound like the kid she remembered.

"Mom, it's Fischer. I can't talk long, we're at a pay phone, but I wanted to call you before we head into the woods. We'll be camping till late tomorrow night, but I'll be checking messages at David's to see when I've officially become a brother. Listen, we're fine, okay? Just take care of yourself." He was suddenly flooded with emotion and had to pause for a moment. "I'll see you soon. Bye."

He hung up the phone and entered the store. Two bikers paid their bill at the counter. Fischer saw his reflection in the circular mirror at the ceiling. In it, he saw the biker wearing a red bandanna knotted over the sleeve of his jacket eyeing him.

"Will that be all?" the clerk behind the counter asked with uninterest. A cigarette had burned down to almost nothing in an ashtray near her elbow and was now emitting a pungent, sickening odor.

The biker turned away and took out his billfold, and that was when Fischer saw the television set mounted on a platform directly above containers of pickle relish and ketchup and mustard. On the screen was a helicopter view of a flooded town.

Last night's storms wreaked havoc on central South Dakota. Here a waterlogged Reliance, South Dakota, where the swollen Missouri River overflowed its banks, covering the town in several feet of water.

The picture changed, and Fischer immediately recognized the town where they had stayed the night before, the jackknifed truck that had burst into flames.

David strolled down the aisle toward Fischer, balancing hot dogs. He gave one to Fischer, then frowned. "What's your problem?" he asked, shoving a hot dog into his mouth. "You look even weirder than usual."

Thistle appeared from the rest room, her face scrubbed clean and her hair damp around her forehead. She noticed the TV at the same time as David.

Scenes from nearby Dothan, South Dakota, where this truck, presumably seeking an alternate route to the city because of flooding, slammed into a building in downtown. It seems the driver suffered a heart attack, but two witnesses managed to pull him from behind the wheel. The man is being treated at St. Jude's Hospital in Rapid City.

Fischer whirled around. David had stopped chewing and was staring at the screen.

David threw the rest of his hot dog onto the counter, and Fischer saw a tiny muscle quiver in his jaw. For the first time ever, Fischer realized, he was witnessing what it was like to see David really afraid. "The truth, Thistle. That guy wasn't chasing Fischer or me, was he?"

Thistle spoke in a low voice. "He cannot hurt us now."

"Calm down, David." Fischer looked around nervously. He was aware that the clerk who had counted out the biker's change was glancing in their direction. But before he could say anything more, David backed away and darted out the front door.

"Hey," the clerk shouted. "Come back! You didn't pay for that food."

Fischer glanced at Thistle, fished some change from his

pocket, and tossed it on the counter, then shoved out the door. He and Thistle were halfway across the parking lot before the door banged shut, their arms and legs becoming a crazy windmill of shadows as they sprinted after David.

/ / /

Rapid City

Convenience Store

Television Set

July 13

2:00 P.M.

This is a special weather advisory for the Rapid City, Spearfish, and Sturgis areas till midnight. Baseball-size hail has been reported widespread, and lightning-producing storms have settled over most of the area. Citizens are advised to stay inside and to take appropriate precautions in the event that these storms should produce funnel clouds similar to those that spawned dozens of tornadoes over the last forty-eight hours. We will continue to broadcast warnings and sightings throughout the afternoon and early evening.

/ / /

To every thing there is a season, and a
time to every purpose under the heaven: A
time to be born, and a time to die; a time
to plant and a time to pluck up that which
is planted.   —*Ecclesiastes 3:1–2*

CHAPTER FIFTEEN

By the time Fischer and Thistle convinced David to stop, thick raindrops fell, and they had lost sight of the highway. The city was a maze of chain-link fences and streets and squat office buildings that all looked the same and never seemed to end. To make matters worse, when Fischer opened his backpack to take a look at the map, he discovered it was missing. Panicked, he emptied every pouch of his pack and the pockets of his jeans but turned up nothing.

"It's gone," he said. "The map is gone."

"And I suppose somehow that's my fault, too," David said.

Fischer wanted to tell David that it *was* his fault, that he'd overreacted and run from the store and left Fischer and Thistle with no option but to do the same. Now the map had been lost. But he said nothing.

Thistle stood. "Do you suppose that Solomon and I travel by map? The sun and the stars can guide us."

But David was no longer listening. His attention was focused on a police car that had stopped at the end of the next block.

Fischer stared, locked in place. Were the police looking for them? He doubted it, unless the convenience store owner had decided David's quick exit was suspicious. Just in case, Fischer considered their possibilities. To his right was a postage stamp yard. To his left, a warehouse with For Lease signs taped to the windows. His mind shifted back to the yard, which abutted a long line of antiquated frame houses. They could run between them if it came to that, but his real concern was that David might panic and run anyway.

But the policeman had spotted them, so they would have to take that chance. A moment later a sprinkling of rain began, and the cruiser rolled up beside them.

"How's it going?" the policeman asked.

Out of the corner of his eye Fischer saw David take a step back. He shielded his eyes and moved beside him. "Fine."

"You live around here?" the policeman asked.

Thistle nodded.

"Then what are the backpacks for?"

"We went camping with some friends, but the weather

wasn't exactly cooperative." Fischer looked down at his muddy jeans and shoes, and the policeman smiled.

"I'd say you kids were lucky if you found cover during those storms last night." His gaze flickered over to David.

Fischer could practically feel David's desire to get away, but at that moment the rain suddenly began to fall harder, turning the sidewalk a darker shade of gray.

"Jeeeez." The policeman looked up at the sky. "Here we go again." He began to roll up his window, then stopped. "Hey, you want a lift home?"

"No, thanks," Fischer said. "We're just around the corner."

"Better make it fast." The policeman pulled away, and the three of them darted down the sidewalk as a forceful rain drummed down.

In a rusted toolshed at the back of someone's house, they took cover to wait out the storm. Fischer dried his face with a dirty T-shirt and Thistle searched through her pack for food, but David, dripping and pale, remained in the doorway of the shed, staring out past the street where water rushed debris along the gutters and into whirlpools that swirled above the flooded drains.

David will be fine once I get him home, Fischer thought. But David looked different somehow, sick maybe. His skin had the pallor of chalk, and it seemed as though his gaze were focused on some distant place that neither Fischer nor Thistle saw.

"Sturgis isn't far." Fischer tried to sound reassuring. "And then it's just a little farther to Castle Rock." He had looked at the map enough times to memorize that much. "I'm guessing it's no more than an hour and a half. If we can find a ride. Can you make it, David?"

"Oh, sure, I can make it." David's face tightened with anger. "But then I'm not the problem. No one is looking for me."

Thistle lowered her eyes and refastened the straps of her pack with a fierce yank, but Fischer knew that there was no mistaking David's resentment of her now.

It was dusk when they finally arrived at an endless terrain of houses. Fischer asked directions from a road crew clearing trees and branches that had fallen during the storm, and one of them pointed in the direction of the highway. David's face seemed to fluctuate between flushed and waxen, his skin damp with something other than the fine mist that made a silvery web on Thistle's hair. As the rain began to fall again, Fischer's hopes did, too. Then suddenly a car pulled up to the red light where they waited, and a young woman in a T-shirt rolled down the window of a Honda.

"Bad night to be waiting for someone," she said.

Fischer walked over to the car. "Yeah," he said. "Looks like our ride ditched us."

"Well, where are you headed?" The woman pushed her chin-length hair behind her ear, exposing triple gold earrings. "I'll give you a lift if you're going toward Sturgis."

Fischer glanced back at Thistle, who shrugged. At the curb David was sullen, staring off into space. Fischer felt a strange feeling of foreboding as he looked at the woman, but hadn't he had felt the same way talking with the policeman? That had turned out to be nothing. Besides, the sooner they got some sleep, the better. Fischer smiled and nodded. "A ride would be great."

A moment later David slid into the front seat, and Fischer and Thistle settled into the back.

"So where've you been?" The woman pulled down the street. "Do you believe this weather? I can't fathom trying to walk anywhere today."

"Yeah," David said. "I should have known better." He looked out the window, and the woman turned her attention to Thistle and Fischer in the rearview mirror.

"Bet I know what you've been up to." She gave them a sly look.

Fischer stopped breathing for a single second. He felt Thistle's hand grip his arm.

"Hiking at Black Hills, right?"

"Exactly," Fischer said. He placed his hand over Thistle's, and felt her fingers relax.

The woman turned her gaze to Thistle. "I can't believe that you didn't get in the middle of those twisters."

"Yes, we were fortunate indeed," Thistle said.

Fischer leaned forward. "She's not from around here," he explained.

"Uh-huh." But the woman's eyes remained on Thistle's face for another long moment.

Fischer looked out the window as they followed the white reflector lights onto the highway. Was he really more at ease, or was it more what David had said that morning, was he just bone tired? Still, the warm car could not have been more luxurious if it had been a limousine. He let his worries about David retreat with the last suburbs of Rapid City.

As they passed under the first exit sign for Sturgis, Fischer shook David's shoulder.

David grunted his response.

"Just a couple of miles," the woman said. "Where should I let you out?"

Fischer hadn't expected the question. "Anywhere is fine."

"Is the statue okay?"

Fischer nodded. "The statue is perfect."

He thought the woman's eyes lingered a moment too long on his before she turned her attention back to the road, but he seemed to have suspicions about everything now. A few minutes later the car left the highway, and they entered a small town that resembled the set of an old western movie. In the center streetlamps were lit, and the slick roads reflected the headlights of the car. Fairy lights strung over the streets blew in wild gusts of wind. The woman pulled up to a square, but when Fischer looked around, he didn't see a statue, and his first prickle of fear registered.

David reached over to open the front door of the car, but the woman placed her hand on top of his and turned off the engine.

"Look, this isn't where you live, is it? You're not from around here, either."

David's eyes widened with panic. The windows of the car had begun to fog slightly, making the town outside seem almost imaginary. Alarm sounded inside Fischer, loud and clanging. He flung open his door and grabbed Thistle's hand, pulling her across the seat and outside with him.

"David, get out," he demanded.

The woman swept her hair behind her ear, and the light of the overhead mirror revealed a scar on her palm. Fischer hurried around the side of the car and opened David's door.

"What's your rush?" the woman asked. She leaned over David and stared up at Fischer with eyes as red as laser lights.

Fischer grabbed his cousin's wrist, but David shook it free. "No rush," he said. He seemed to be hypnotized as Fischer pulled him off the car seat and shoved him toward Thistle.

"Go," Fischer ordered. "Move. Now."

Thistle yanked David's arm and pulled him across the square.

"The Stones are not yours," the woman told Fischer. "You've made a grave mistake, but it's not too late to rectify the matter."

Fischer backed away.

"Come with me now. It doesn't have to hurt," she said.

The words had a familiar ring. They were almost identical to the words of the man who had hunted Fischer behind David's house in the woods.

"He's coming," the woman said. "You can't get away. He'll find you."

Fischer was tired. Too much effort. He looked up at the lights. Were there stars behind his eyes?

"You're weary." The woman's words were a lullaby. "So weary. There's the girl, your cousin, and what's this?" She narrowed her eyes. "Your mother and a new child."

There was some thought that was trying to surface, but it all seemed so far away. He closed his eyes and saw the Shadowy Figure. Then a flood of light wiped that image clean, and suddenly it was Grandpa's face he saw.

"Fischer, wake up." Grandpa was smiling from the doorway of the room that Fischer slept in when he stayed with him. "Get up, pal. It's time to get a move on."

Fischer opened his eyes and forced himself to break the woman's stare. "You can't have her," he said. "I'll never let you have Thistle."

"Silly boy." The woman smiled as she leaned further toward him and whispered, "It's you he wants."

For this is he, of whom it is written,
Behold, I send my messenger before
thy face, which shall prepare thy way
before thee. —Matthew 11:10

CHAPTER SIXTEEN

As they moved along the shoulders of the road, spruces heavy with rain showered down and sent the sharp scent of pine into the air. Even David seemed to sense an urgency and was moving more quickly now. Fischer stopped more than once at the sound of breaking branches in the underbrush. He froze in fear as a pair of glowing eyes peered through the trees, only to come face-to-face with an elk that crossed their path and continued into the blackness.

"We're lost, aren't we?" David asked.

Fischer stopped in his tracks. They had run for a long time, and the lights of Sturgis had disappeared. Despite exhaustion, the words of the woman in the car spurred him on. It's *you* he wants. He tried to force himself to think about where they were, but he could not get the woman's threat out of his head.

"Admit it, Fischer." David dropped his backpack to his

feet and sat down in the middle of the road. "You have no clue where we are."

It was true. And now, enveloped in darkness, and with no hint of the rain letting up, Fischer began to have the feeling that they were fumbling along for nothing, that they were already defeated but hadn't mustered the courage to admit it.

He walked ahead, trying to shake his gloom, and suddenly the same sensation of vertigo he had felt staring into the lamp in David's hallway overtook him. He stopped, his head spinning, as images materialized and hurtled past him: the Shadowy Figure, Thistle, David, his mother, then the figure of a lone man in the desert. And flashes from his dreams: running through the meadow, the man from the campfire gaining, standing to face him with a glowing Stone in his palm. At last he saw the two-lane road where he now stood and a trail that twisted into deeper woods.

Fischer opened his eyes and walked forward with purpose. Only a hundred feet ahead he discovered an opening that separated the tall grass at the roadside, and all at once there it was: the same trail he had seen in his vision just moments ago.

David caught up first. "You expect me to go in there?"

"It's safer than staying on this road," Fischer said.

David hesitated. "If it weren't for Thistle," he said, poking a finger into Fischer's chest, "none of this would be happening. She's the reason we're in this mess."

Fischer frowned. "We're in this mess because I took the Stones."

"You sound brainwashed. Correction: You are. I've seen the way you look at her. She has you exactly where she wants you." David paused. "But you're not fooling me, Fischer. If I'm worried, deep down you must be petrified." David turned away as Thistle caught up, and again Fischer sensed that the fate of their trip hung by the thinnest thread.

What Fischer hadn't told David was that he had no idea where they were headed or how far out of the way this path might take them. He only knew that the trail had been revealed in a vision and that his instincts told him to trust, move forward, while his brain fought and tried to convince him otherwise. As they climbed each height, rounded each switchback, he looked for a safe place to spend the night, anything that resembled a shelter. Finally the trail opened and spilled out of the woods into a wide, grassy clearing.

"I think this is it," Fischer said.

"About time." David threw down his pack, and Thistle caught Fischer's eye. They had listened to David grouse about his blistered feet and wet clothes since they left the road, but now Fischer's patience was wearing thin.

"I'll make some tea," Thistle said, casting David a look of controlled patience. "Maybe that will improve your humor."

Fischer was numb with exhaustion as they shook out their sleeping bags and searched for sticks, but within a half hour a campfire was going, more smoke than blaze, but still a fire. Water was heated, and Thistle took a pouch from her pack and steeped some dried leaves. She turned with the first steaming cup, but David was already sprawled, snoring, on his sleeping bag.

Fischer sat down next to Thistle at the campfire. He wanted to sleep, but he knew what he would see if he closed his eyes, so he tried to resist. He remembered the words of the woman in the car, and instantly his eyes snapped open.

"Your cousin David is not as resilient as I once thought." Thistle gave Fischer a cup of tea. It smelled like summer flowers. "He seems unfamiliar with hardship."

"That's an understatement," Fischer said. "But it's not David I'm worried about." The truth was, he was glad to have David asleep so that he could speak freely with Thistle. "It's the woman, the one in the car. Something she told me."

Thistle frowned and leaned forward. "Then out with it at once."

"She said *I'm* the one they're looking for."

"You?" Thistle rose to her feet.

Fischer's voice became thin. "Is it true?"

"So. They believe that you still possess the Stones." Thistle stared beyond the firelight.

A shadow passed over her face, like the one Fischer had seen the first morning at David's house, when she had accused him of hiding more than the two Stones he'd admitted. But as quickly as it had appeared, the shadow vanished.

"My fears have been well founded," she said. "We are all in danger. If Belial's minions think that you are now the one who holds the Stones, I assure you, they will not stop looking for you until the Taker's Stones are found."

Fischer suddenly felt sick. "But even if they caught us, they wouldn't find the Stones they're looking for. They'd let us go, wouldn't they?"

Thistle squeezed her hands together, then held them near the fire. "Belial showed my mother no mercy when he found her."

Fischer didn't really want to know more, yet he felt that he had to ask. "How did she die?"

Thistle broke a branch into kindling before she began to speak. "I was a very small child. As I have told you, we lived in a cottage in the mountains. On this particular day in the year 1811 my father was called to consult with one of the priests, and I was asked to help the nuns of the church with their duties while my mother stayed home.

"But while I was at the monastery, I fell and cut my ankle in the garden. Before my eyes the wound closed into the scar of the half heart—the Keepers' mark—though at the time I did not know that. It was such a queer thing, the scar, that I showed it to one of the nuns. I will never forget her expression upon seeing it, and within moments the entire monastery was alerted. A party was sent to our cottage, and they brought back the fateful news. In our absence my mother had fallen victim to an arrow."

"But wait a minute," Fischer said. "You said the Keepers were safe for three days from the time they were separated. At least if they had all the Stones."

Thistle's voice was strained as she turned toward the fire. "Yes, but unbeknownst to my father and mother, a Stone had been stolen from my mother's pouch that very morning. When the pouch was retrieved, only one Stone was missing—the Taker's Stone—and so the rest were rendered useless. Still, Belial somehow knew the Stones were separated. He was also aware that with one gone, my mother was left vulnerable, and so he urged his marked ones to seek her out and kill her."

"What happened to the missing Stone?" Fischer asked. "It must have eventually been found—"

"Yes." Thistle whirled around to face him. Was it pain or anger he saw gleaming in her eyes? "And returned to Solomon along with the pouch of Stones that Rosemary had managed to hide. That same day the priests secreted me away for fear that Belial's men would destroy me."

"So you and Solomon split up," Fischer said. "But wait. Didn't the world go nuts, like it's going crazy now?"

"Truly, it did." Thistle shrugged and dropped to the

ground beside him. "Until I took my place as the Second Keeper."

Fischer felt as though the past had suddenly reached out and touched his present. "But you were a kid."

"I was chosen," Thistle said simply. "I bore the scar of the divided heart. A few short days later my image appeared on the white stone, and so it was decided. Though I was very young at the time, I left the protection of the Rom who had agreed to conceal me." As Thistle stared into the fire, her eyes clouded. She drew up her legs and rested her cheek on her knees. "You may not understand this duty I feel, Fischer. But I will always be Keeper first, I must, even if I am never anything more. Those times will always be painful to recall. They are cast in shadows because a light was forever taken from me when my dear mother was killed."

That's enough, Fischer thought, that's all she can stand to tell and all I want to know, but his mind seemed locked onto Thistle's story. Until now, he had found the past in books, in the artifacts he and his mother cataloged for the museum. When he was absorbed in those things, the past became large, and the present receded, as though each was seen through opposite ends of a telescope. But now he saw that by his taking the stones, elements of history had overlapped into his own life.

And Thistle's? He pressed his fists together and held them to his mouth. The last time a Stone had been taken, her world had been turned upside down. Now he was the Taker. She had every reason to hate him.

"If I could, I'd change all this." Fischer dropped his hands helplessly and stood. "If I'd known—I would never have touched those Stones."

He couldn't look at her now, knowing what she must think of him. As he began to turn away, she reached up and grasped his arm. "Do you recall what I told you that first day, Fischer? The Stones return to each owner a share of himself. So I can only think that your request brought me here because somehow, in the threads of your life and mine, we are not tangled, but tied." She pulled him down beside her, then took his hand between her own. Her eyes were shining in the light of the fire. "And, after all your efforts to bring me safely to my father, Fischer, how could I believe you are anything but my dearest friend?"

Thistle smiled, and Fischer wished he could muster the nerve to say what he believed, that he had never met anyone as wise, as kind, and as beautiful, that he didn't understand how he could ever deserve the tenderness he read in her eyes. But no matter what he said, the facts remained the same.

Thistle gently let go of Fischer's hand and stood to empty the rest of her tea onto the fire. "We must rest."

Fischer spread out his sleeping bag as Thistle stretched out on her own and looked up at the sky. "Try to sleep now, put away your fears. All things serve a purpose."

"All things, like Keepers and Takers?"

"I suppose my own destiny is clear," Thistle said. "But though yours is unknown, still it is there, waiting." She closed her eyes, her voice already fading into sleep. "Look, Fischer. All around this place, it rains, it floods, the winds howl, but here there are only stars. You have chosen well."

Fischer looked up at the clear sky that had appeared as the clouds drew away. He was afraid to close his eyes and afraid to leave them open. The words of the woman in the car played over and over in his head, and he couldn't make them stop. He wasn't sure anymore what was real and what wasn't. And knowing that, how could he ever sleep?

/ / /

Please be advised that fluctuations in temperatures and conditions in the Black Hills vicinity are now considered dangerous. Heavy rains have been reported in lower local regions, and our central office has received reports of sleet and hail from the Devil's Tower area in Wyoming and east to Spearfish. All park visitors should be signed in and out of ranger stations until otherwise advised. Please inform campers and hikers who choose to proceed with foot travel that extreme caution should be exercised due to the continued threat of rapidly deteriorating conditions.

/ / /

Am I my brother's keeper?——Genesis 4:9

CHAPTER SEVENTEEN

Fischer had tossed and turned all through the night and was relieved when at last daylight began to make a silhouette of the trees and the horizon. He discovered that they had spent the night not in a field at all, but on a leveled-off portion of some great bank. He kicked out of his sleeping bag, grabbed the jacket he had used for a pillow, and walked to an overlook occupied by a single yellow-skinned pine.

Behind him was the slope they had taken from Sturgis, now miles away, while in front of him a gigantic mountain of rock rose above the grass and prairie. He spotted another path below him and scrambled down to reach it, hoping to determine what place they had stumbled upon in the darkness. Farther below, where the slope dwindled into flatlands, tour buses were pulling into a paved parking area. Fischer began to walk and several minutes later found a brass plaque set in rock.

WELCOME TO BEAR BUTTE,
SACRED MOUNTAIN OF THE PLAINS INDIAN
Many Indians today continue to have faith in the
beliefs of natural power in the universe and they
recognize the similarity between their Great Spirit
and the God of the white man. Please respect the
beliefs of the Indian people who visit Bear Butte
to pray and fast. Leave prayer cloths and other
Indian religious articles in place. Thank you.

The call of a bobwhite broke the stillness, and Fischer
started back up the path toward the clearing where he had
left Thistle and David sleeping. Something in the trees
caught his eye: strips of cloth and pouches tied to the low
branches of the pines, probably the prayer cloths he had
read about on the marker. All at once he felt a familiar
ache of sadness as he remembered the candles Grandpa
had sometimes lighted as a kind of prayer.

Then Fischer recalled a day he'd spent with Grandpa, a
day last March, when his father had flown out on his latest
overseas assignment. Fischer and Grandpa had gone on
one of their long walks together. Fischer was brooding,
wondering what kind of assignment, military or otherwise,
could possibly make his father want to leave his mother
and him behind again. But he was also furious with himself
for caring. Hadn't his father made it clear enough on this
visit home that Fischer would never measure up? Fischer

wouldn't be class president if he didn't become more out-spoken, wouldn't make friends if he refused to take up new interests, wouldn't be the athlete that David was until he made an effort to overcome his clumsiness. The coldness of Fischer's last awkward handshake with his father at the airport was indelibly imprinted on his mind.

But when Grandpa and Fischer reached the center of town, they had walked up to a great stone church and Grandpa had pulled Fischer through a massive doorway so that he could light a candle. "For your father," Grandpa had told him. But Fischer had refused to take part. He stormed off to wait on one of the cool pews of the old church, thinking the smell of the place was queer with its mustiness and incense and lemon oil.

Indistinguishable shapes moved outside the leaded win-dows, and only the popping sound of wooden beams ex-panding in the heat broke the silence. But then Fischer had begun to feel peaceful. He had the sense that if he only stretched out on the pews and gave himself up to the sounds and the smell of that place, his anger and grief would fall away. When he looked up, the sun through the stained glass windows became warm on his face. Its light illuminated the figures in the parables, making them ap-pear to flicker to life for the sole purpose of his comfort. Moments later Fischer was lulled into a calm so deep that when Grandpa returned and saw Fischer's face, he could only remark, "What happened to you?"

Now Fischer shielded his eyes against the emerging sun and watched the branches filled with prayer cloths gently wave in the morning breeze. He pulled off his jacket and ripped the cuff from his shirt. He tied it to a tiny shrub of misshapen pine that had sprung from a crack in an immense rock. But a moment later he felt the strange vertigo sensation again.

Then the image of the Shadowy Figure emerged, flooded by a great light, and he saw another man, a man Fischer recognized as Thistle's father. He was lying on his blanket, asleep, with the pouch cinched at the waist of his robe, just as he had been the night that Fischer had been at his campfire. Fischer saw himself as he slipped from behind the tree and crawled forward. He reached Solomon's blanket and shook the Stones into his hand. But at that moment Thistle turned in her sleep, startling him. Some Stones fell onto the blanket, and Fischer shoved the rest into his jacket pocket. But before he did, Fischer saw his hand close over *three*.

Fischer's eyes sprang open. He sank to the ground beside the path and tried to control his heartbeat, tapping rapid-fire under his ribs. But how could it be? Had he lost a Stone in the woods or at the stream where he had fallen? He squeezed his eyes closed again, but all he could see now was the last piece of his vision: his own hand, holding three stones.

Fischer opened his eyes and began to search everywhere: his jeans pockets, his shirt. He pulled off his hiking boots and socks and emptied dirt onto the path. Was it possible somehow he still had one of the Stones? If he did, it could be anywhere: back at the campfire, hidden in his backpack, in his sleeping bag, or even back at White Horse, in the woods. He looked away in frustration. Then his eyes fixed on his jacket, his favorite one, lying beside him. He snatched it up and shoved his hand into the pockets.

He had worn the jacket the night he had taken the Stones from the pouch. He had run, the Stones safe in his front pocket, across the fields, through the woods, tripping at the creek, yet he hadn't found any when he went back to look for them. He could almost convince himself that he had dropped one—that someone else had found it—but that wouldn't explain why the woman in the car had told him that he was the one being searched for, it wouldn't explain the fact that they were still being hunted. Thistle had been right all along: He must still have a Stone.

Fischer's fingertips touched something hard under the front pocket. Barely breathing, he discovered a hole in the fabric. Something lay underneath, inside the lining, and after a moment of probing and shaking, Fischer dragged a smooth object from inside. An electric tingle passed through him as he held it up between two fingers to the yellow light of day, admiring its brilliance. As a wave of emotion shook him, the Stone glowed a deep scarlet. Fischer tried to rise to his feet. It was his; he hadn't lost it. The third Stone was his.

Fischer stood, rejuvenated now that the Stone was in his grasp. He had not felt so clearheaded since they left White Horse, never so strong or so sure. And why shouldn't he feel that way now? He had found them a place to rest the night. David had been no help at all. And Thistle spoke of destiny; somehow this Stone was his. He felt a pain where his hand gripped it. But if he told Thistle about the third Stone, she would never believe that he hadn't known all along. Perhaps she would think that he had hidden it away from her, that he couldn't be trusted. He wasn't about to take that chance and lose her now. He would see her safely to Solomon and then give her back the missing Stone. He would explain how he'd seen it in a vision and found it. Would it matter that he hadn't told her right away?

"Where have you been?" David stood over him at the top of the slope. "I've been looking all over for you."

Fischer folded his hand over the Stone and stuffed it into his jacket pocket. "Just getting our bearings."

"That doesn't exactly sound promising." David picked his way down the hill. "So where are we?"

"A place called Bear Butte," Fischer said. He remembered David's words from the night before and wondered what he should say to clear the air between them. "You seem better."

"I slept for once." David rubbed his temples and pulled his sunglasses down from the top of his head. "Now if I could only lose this headache."

"I don't think we have more than another forty, fifty miles. See those buses?" Fischer asked, pointing to the tour buses below. "We'll find out where they're headed and take whichever will get us closest to Castle Rock and—"

"And nothing," David said, yanking his glasses off again. "We've brought Thistle this far and have risked our necks doing it. Enough is enough." David stared at Fischer, searching for something, perhaps a gesture, a nod of agreement. When Fischer remained motionless, David stuffed the sunglasses in his T-shirt pocket and snatched up a rock from the ground. "Look, Thistle is as good as there. Now let's start using our heads, okay? My vote is to put her on that bus and send her on her way. In a couple of hours she'll be in Castle Rock and we'll be headed home. It makes sense; you know it does. All we have to do is tell her, together, that's how it's going to be."

Fischer looked David squarely in the eye. "I wouldn't do that to Thistle."

"But you'd do that to me?" David suddenly whirled around and hurled the rock as far as he could into the distance. "I'm your own flesh and blood; I'm family. She's nobody." He turned back to Fischer and pushed back his hair, dusted off his hands. "Look, we've done enough. I want to go home, I want things to fall back into place. Remember? The way they were before."

As Fischer met David's gaze, he didn't like what he saw, something cold and distant glinting behind his eyes. Fischer could guess what David wanted. He wanted Fischer to be on his side, to tell him that he was right, that they would return to what they'd been, cousins, maybe even fellow adventurers, so long as David was the one to call the shots.

He wanted Fischer to say okay, he'd leave Thistle behind, and then forget he'd ever met her. Only Fischer knew he couldn't, wouldn't. If there were miracles in the world, then Thistle was his. And now that he felt what it was like to care for someone, to have her care about him, he was changed. He was never again going to be the Fischer David remembered. So he remained silent till David seemed to read all this in his expression and turned away.

"My head is killing me." David started up the slope. "I've got to get some aspirin."

Fischer cast a final glance toward the parking lots below, then headed back toward the clearing where they had spent the night. They should move on while the weather held.

Thistle seemed to follow Fischer's lead, wolfing down a quick breakfast before they broke camp. David seemed agitated, his fingers fumbling as they tied the sleeping bags onto their packs. He said nothing but walked far out in front as they made their way down the long path from the ridge into the parking area. By the time they arrived at the buses, an assortment of people with cameras and binoculars were gathering beside them.

"Everyone on the Black Hills tour, time to board," a man called from the stairs of the first bus. "Next stop Spearfish. Another bus will depart in an hour to Rapid City."

Thistle spoke to one of the tourists, then reported back. "The Spearfish bus is the one that will bring us closest to Castle Rock," she said.

"Okay," Fischer said. "But there's a problem. We won't exactly blend into this crowd with backpacks and sleeping bags."

Thistle nodded. "We should leave them behind. They'll serve little purpose now—"

"Wait a minute," David interrupted. "I'm not leaving my pack. That stuff is all we've got."

"We don't need the packs. Remember, we've still got money," Fischer said.

"No, we don't," David snapped. "I had our money in my backpack yesterday, but when I checked this morning, it was gone."

"What?" Fischer was not at all sure he believed David, though why he would lie about this, Fischer didn't know. "You lost it? And you didn't tell us?"

Thistle turned to David. "Leave your pack. As I said, it is of little consequence. Solomon will see you safely home."

"And how will he do that? With his magic wand?" David turned his back on them, and Fischer had the recurring sensation that his world was a millimeter away from being toppled. "Do what you want, but I've made up my mind. I'm not going."

Thistle froze.

"You don't mean that," Fischer said, but he knew that David did.

"Don't you get it, Fish? When she goes, if she even finds this guy Solomon, we've got nothing but our tickets to get back. We'll have no money, no packs. Don't forget my folks will be home in White Horse tomorrow night. If we're not back there—"

"But we will be," Fischer told him.

"And as I told you," Thistle said, "my father will gladly—"

"Look." David cut her off with a wave of his hands. "Your father is your father. But we don't know anything about the guy, Fish. And after what's happened, I wonder if he even exists. I'm not so sure what I believe."

"Well, I'm sure," Fischer said. He leveled his gaze at David. "I believe Thistle."

David's eyes smoldered. "We could be left in the middle of nowhere or worse."

"No," Fischer said.

"Do what you want." David shrugged. "Like I said, I'm not going. I'll take the other bus back to the airport and wait for you. By myself, I doubt I'll be followed."

Fischer stared at his cousin, who had already dropped his pack onto the grass and sat down. Behind them the bus engine started with a rumble.

"Fine," Fischer said. "I'll find you at the airport tonight."

"What if you're not there?" David avoided looking at Thistle.

Fischer watched as Thistle unfastened her backpack and, taking out a T-shirt, quickly wrapped the silver knife and scabbard she had brought from White Horse in it. He felt fear rising, but pushed it down.

"If I'm not, then leave. Go home without me." Fischer pulled the last of the food from his pack, hesitating before he stood to join Thistle. He had hoped David might change his mind, but now he could see he wasn't going to. David stared straight ahead, his mouth set, his arms locked around his knees. For a moment Fischer fluctuated between sadness and disbelief, but that gave way to another emotion as dark and furious as a nest of hornets. "Come on, Thistle," he said, taking her arm. "We'd better go."

Fischer and Thistle fell in with the crowds beside the bus and boarded. Someone turned and spoke to Fischer in another language. As he and Thistle slid into the back row of the bus, Fischer spotted David from the window. He had stretched out on the grass, one arm draped over his face. The gulf between him and David seemed too wide ever to close. Tears sprang to Fischer's eyes, but he shoved his fist under his chin and blinked them back. What would happen to him, to all of them? The bus began to roll away from the parking area.

"Only about a half hour, folks, to the beautiful western town of Spearfish. Most of the movie *Dances with Wolves* was filmed in this area."

Fischer stared at the tour guide as he spoke, not hearing the words. It was up to only him now, and Thistle. Then he remembered the Stone in his pocket. He could have told David about it. Maybe it would have even convinced David to come, but he hadn't.

"Thistle?"

She lifted her head from the seat back.

"Do the Stones—can they do *anything?*"

Thistle blinked and frowned. Her thoughts seemed far away. "The Stones can do many things." She looked out the window at Bear Butte as the bus roared down the road. The sky was darkening in the direction they were headed. "Their power is immeasurable, but there is one quality the Stones possess that men do not consider."

Fischer felt a chill. "And what's that?"

"Although the Keepers are immune to the power of the Stones, others are not." Thistle studied Fischer. "Because of their very nature, the Stones play with hearts. They sway men between Light and Dark. They can torture the soul and cause great anguish."

Fischer nodded as she finished. He was afraid if he said any more, he would give himself away.

Thistle gave him a dim smile before she turned to look out the window. Outside lightning flicked at the horizon like the forked tongues of serpents.

Fischer rolled the Stone inside his pocket. He felt a rush of excitement, a thrill as tangible as when he had first seen the Stones in Solomon's hand. How could he bear to be without it? He tried to convince himself that his silence could protect Thistle, that if whoever was looking for them found them again, he might need the Stone for leverage. In the meantime, inside his palm, the Stone was warm and safe.

David resents what I've become, he thought. I'm the leader now. That's why he didn't come.

Fischer grasped the Stone, his head soaring with satisfaction, while above a clatter like the sound of spilled marbles heralded a sudden downpour of hail.

*And many false prophets shall rise, and
shall deceive many.* —*Matthew 24:11*

CHAPTER EIGHTEEN

The cashier at the Sunrise Café, Annie Rae Wilbanks, watched the morning sky out the window turn into a bruise in the direction of Spearfish. When she leaned against her lone Skylark in the parking lot during her ten o'clock break, the air was stone still, as if the sky might be holding its breath. Not a single car had passed in the fifteen minutes she stood outside.

Now it was past eleven, and Annie Rae had decided that Connie, her relief waitress, was not coming in. She would have to handle the lunch crowd and the cash register herself. Not that there would be a lunch crowd today. The Sunrise picked up the trade traffic during the week, the construction guys, park service people, and linemen who worked in either Spearfish or Belle Fourche. But between the weather's brewing something ugly and its being Saturday, Annie Rae figured no one to show.

She was changing the display case from doughnuts to a

couple of oozing pieces of lemon meringue pie when she heard the bell above the door ring. A man stood at the entrance of the cafe. He was dressed in dark clothes that set off dark hair, burned butter eyes, and the kind of skin that was too smooth for him to have lived in Dakota long. He took off his coat, and she watched his long hands arrange it on the coatrack. Annie Rae always looked at hands. They told so much about a person. She adjusted her skirt and hoped her nose had not gone oily over the heat of the grill top.

"Cup of coffee?" Annie Rae called out to the man.

The man didn't answer. He looked around the place as though he planned to buy it. For all she knew, he would. Might be one of those guys her boss, Dewey, claimed would dance in here one of these days, plunk down some cash, and make all his dreams come true.

Annie Rae poured a cup of coffee and walked toward the man. She handed him the steaming mug. He took it, then held it as though doing so were a nuisance, the way single men held babies when they were handed to them unexpectedly.

"Some sky out there," she said. "I didn't see a car pull in. Where'd you come from?"

"I come from dust," the man said, turning to face her with his strangely smooth face. He produced a toothy smile, which Annie Rae tried to equal though her own teeth were slightly yellow with cigarette stains.

"Don't you like my coffee?" she asked.

The man walked around the room. He picked up the sugar canisters and held them at eye level. When Annie Rae turned to wipe the counters, he sniffed the catsup bottle before setting it down again. Then he studied his fingernails, and his forehead furrowed.

"Come on over here and sit down," Annie Rae said, stuffing the rag somewhere under the counter. "I haven't had a soul to talk to all morning. And you're more interesting than most we get in this place."

The man sat on the stool beside her and looked into her eyes. He was flat gorgeous with his tenor voice and his dark-as-soot hair, almost like fur. Maybe if he hung around town long enough, he'd ask her out. She could use a man with some class, and this one reeked of it.

"I know what you're up to, you know," Annie Rae said. She clicked a coral-colored nail against her capped front tooth.

The man returned the untouched cup of coffee to the counter. "Do you?"

"You're planning to buy the place, right?" Annie Rae said. "Dewey told you the place was plum, and you took the bite."

"What is this?" the man asked, taking her hand into his own to study the tiny diamond she had glued to her index fingernail.

Annie Rae laughed. "That's my play pretty," she said.

"Somebody once told me it made me look high mainte-nance."

He released her hand, then whisked some stray granules of sugar from the counter and wiped his hands on a nap-kin.

"It disgusts me." The man studied his nails again. "This filth under my nails."

"Oh, but you've got beautiful hands." Annie Rae tenta-tively reached to take his hand in hers. Soft—soft as a baby's. Her fingertips drifted over his knuckles, and she shivered.

Annie Rae reached for her fringed purse and pulled out a nail file. "I did manicures before I came here," she said, her eyes drifting up to the spackled ceiling. She began to run the tip of the file under each of the man's perfect nails. "Don't worry about dirt. You're in South Dakota now. This place was underwater once, you know. After that the dinosaurs took over. You can still find fossils and petrified poop, I'm not kidding. But now look. All that's left is grass and rock and dust and hail, and in the winter, snow past an elephant's butt. Yes, sir," Annie Rae said, finishing the man's nails with a flourish, "welcome to South Dakota."

"I have need of you," the man said, taking Annie Rae's hand again and touching the tiny embedded diamond in her fingernail.

Annie Rae leaned her chin on her free hand. "Music to my ears," she said.

The man traced the veins of her hand with fascination, and Annie Rae felt a little shiver go up her spine. "Look, you going to order?" she asked, pulling her hand away to stand. Suddenly she had the feeling the guy might be playing with her head and not the other way around. "My lunch crowd comes in soon."

"I wonder if you have seen three"—the man seemed to select his words carefully—"youngsters." His eyes settled on hers.

"Has there been some kind of trouble?" she asked.

The man chuckled. "Oh, yes," he said, nodding, "there's been some trouble, Annie Rae."

"How do you know my name?" she asked, moving a step backward.

"I know everyone's name," the man said. He strolled behind the counter. "Everyone who is from dust."

"Hey, you're not supposed to be back here," Annie Rae objected, moving away from the counter toward the door. "If you're from some government agency, I'm going to call the cops. You can't just barge in here and—"

"Such a fragile lot," the man interrupted. "Your words are bold, but your minds are weak." He selected an egg from an open carton by the grill. Suddenly he cracked the egg between two fingers, dropped back his head, and poured the contents into his mouth. She could hear the crunch of the eggshell before he swallowed. "For example, now. *Now* you are frightened, Annie Rae."

Annie Rae was frozen in place, her hand gripping a chair on one of the tables. Suddenly the man's eyes went as red as her apron.

"And you have reason to be," the man said, dabbing his mouth with a silk handkerchief, "if you have knowledge of those children and have not told me."

Annie Rae shook her head, the blood in her veins beating as if it might crack the shell of her own heart. "Look, mister, I haven't seen or heard of any kids around here. I told you. Maybe if I knew what they looked like—"

"Oh, that," the man said. He glanced around the room as if he might ask for volunteers, then turned back to her. Suddenly an image came into her head: two boys and a girl, none of them any older than her sister's teenage kids.

"These are the ones I desire," the man said.

Annie Rae shook her head. "I ain't seen them."

"That's too bad," the man said, taking a toothpick from the dispenser by the register and holding it between his fingers. "But you will let me know if you do, won't you, Annie Rae?"

"Sure I will," Annie Rae whispered, "if you'll leave me your number."

The man reached out and touched her hair. "I've frightened you, yet you're confused. You find me attractive, as I do you. You'd like to be mine, wouldn't you, my angel?"

"Oh, yes." Annie Rae was suddenly breathless.

"But all things come at a price. You know that, don't you?"

Annie Rae nodded, though her head felt as though it were filled with cotton.

The man drew her hand toward his lips and kissed it, then held it tightly between his own.

"Ow," Annie Rae cried out. She looked down at her hand, where a circular burn was blistering on her palm.

"You'll always have that ring, Annie Rae," the man said. "It's my gift to you. Do you like it?"

Annie Rae stroked the mark with her fingernail.

The man smiled and took his coat off the hook. "Now I'm afraid I must go. Business, pressing business."

"No," Annie Rae said, her voice sounding like a child's. In her head she was a little girl, eight, living back in Tacoma.

"Oh, my dear." The man made a clucking sound with his tongue. He fiddled the toothpick between his lips, then threw it away. "You're disappointed. We had so little time." He reached out and stroked Annie Rae's diamond-studded finger.

"But don't fret, my angel," the man said. He smoothed back his hair before he turned away and pulled open the door. "From what I recall of your life, we will have plenty of time to make up for that later."

/ / /

Radio at the Sunrise Café
South Dakota
Saturday, July 14
11:00 P.M.

And now for our local news. In Custer State Park today acres of trees fell for no discernible reason. The president made a nation-wide address this morning in which he declared a national state of emergency in South Dakota following this brutal week of climate-related catastrophes. In the meantime, Custer State Park has been closed, and scientists are planning to move into the park tomorrow to try to solve this most recent and bizarre weather puzzle.

Stay tuned for a late-night report:
Extreme Weather: What's the cause and where will it end? Tonight at eleven-thirty on this broadcast station.

/ / /

Verily, verily, I say unto you, that one of
you shall betray me. —John 13:21

_____

CHAPTER NINETEEN

"Not in all my blessed days." The driver of the semitruck who had picked up Fischer and Thistle outside Spearfish shook his head. "Never have I seen this," he muttered as he steered through the wreckage of jackknifed trucks and cars on the highway. Red and blue flashing lights created an eerie SOS, accompanying the droning howl of sirens. As they passed a stretch of road where the hail had accumulated into an icy slick, the driver glanced over at Fischer. "Listen, I may be crazy to be out here, but a few miles after I drop you two off, I'll be home. So what's your story? What are two kids doing out in the middle of all hell breaking loose?"

Fischer and Thistle exchanged a glance, but Fischer was numb from the sight of the wreckage outside. Tears stung his eyes as he met the driver's gaze. I did this, he silently confessed, me. The man squinted back at him, but of course he couldn't understand, so Fischer turned away to stare out the side window. What seemed like endless hours later, the driver pulled the truck to a halt outside a boxy building with a sign overhead that read SUNRISE CAFÉ.

"This is it," he said. "I'd take you closer to Castle Rock, but this rig wouldn't make it on these secondary roads. I've got to stick to interstate from here on out."

"It's okay," Fischer said. "But how much further do we have to go?"

The driver adjusted his side mirror. "About a mile. But this is the last sign of civilization till you hit Custer State Park. Nothing from here on but ranchland and sky. Look, I don't know what's going on with you two—"

Fischer looked up, alarmed, but the man held up his hand. "I'm not trying to make it my business, all right, but do me a favor: Just sit tight for a while, will you? The hail I've seen today could knock a hole in you, and it looks like the bottom's getting ready to drop out again. Tell Annie Rae that Krausey sent you in to use the phone. She'll take care of you till somebody sends help."

Fischer waved, hot air blasting over him as the rig pulled away. "This is it. Do you want to rest inside before we go on?" he asked Thistle. But then he realized that they couldn't stop. Up until now, despite the hail and the rain, the sky had provided some light, but it was fading fast.

Thistle seemed to share the same thought. "No," she said. As she stared up at the clouds, her face seemed to take on their strange hue. "The time for rest has passed."

The skin on Fischer's arms prickled as lightning shot out of the dark clouds and into the pasture beside them. Rain began to fall in heavy drops.

They started down the road that divided the country-side into matching halves of brown and yellow grassland. In the distance, buttes sprung up from the earth like alien ruins, breaking the granite gray horizon, and Fischer began to feel as he had the first time he turned the handle on a jack-in-the-box, that something was going to happen, something unavoidable, but what?

As they walked, the dark skies turned darker, till only a dim light stretched over the land, and the hour seemed closer to dusk. Thistle proceeded in silence, her expression grim and resigned. Fischer felt for the Stone hidden deep in his pocket, and his apprehension left him as he remembered. With the Stone in his hand, he was capable of anything.

The low grass rippled, giving off a moaning sound as a breeze passed over the sloping hills. When Fischer stopped to look back in the direction they had come, he saw nothing but the deceptive mirage of faraway heat. Or was it oncoming rain? He stopped to clear his head, took a sip from his canteen, and offered some to Thistle. She lifted the metal container to her lips.

But then a sound, one that drowned out the gentle rustling of grass, stirred the air. The canteen fell at Thistle's feet, and Fischer glanced up. The ground at the horizon seemed to shift. It was unfocused in the same undulating way as heat on asphalt, but moving low and horizontally, as if a dam had broken, and water were now racing toward them.

"What is it?" Fischer dropped the Stone he grasped inside his pocket. "Can you tell?"

Thistle took his hand. "He comes."

"Who?" Fischer shouted over the rising noise. "Belial?"

"Listen to me, Fischer. Whatever happens, look ahead and walk on. Remember, Belial will do all he can to deceive you."

Fischer steeled himself. A shudder ran through him.

"Belial," Thistle announced, "we are unafraid."

She pulled Fischer forward as the sound intensified. Hail began to fall as they walked, stinging Fischer's arms, shattering into shards as it hit the hard surface of the road.

"That's all it is," Fischer said. "Hail coming."

"No," Thistle said. "Look forward and hold fast."

Fischer took her hand and grasped it tighter. The sound was deafening yet subtle, causing an unending tingle in his feet and fingertips. What could be making it? He wanted to turn and discover what was there; still, as he made a move, something inside him warned that he wouldn't like what he saw.

"Look ahead, Fischer," Thistle ordered. "Do not look back."

Then, at the ground beside his feet, Fischer felt something sinuous, like muscle, moving beside his heels, between his shoes, then over and around them. Fischer kicked out, and whatever it was darted away.

Now the noise moved ahead of them, and Fischer stopped in place, frozen with fear. As the vibration intensified under his feet, he couldn't help himself: He looked down and then froze, unable to make a single sound or movement. His heart pounded with such effort that he questioned whether he could even breathe. There, in a moving tangle that wove around his ankles and slid over his feet, were snakes—copperheads, rattlers, sidewinders— snakes everywhere.

He would take the Stone from his pocket, wish this away, and save both himself and Thistle. But before he could, Thistle grabbed his hand again.

"Look at me," she said.

He met her eyes and willed his heart to beat slowly, more slowly.

"They are only pawns for Belial. He means to try to frighten you, Fischer. Study the colors above the hills. Gray as the veins in the marble pillars of Rome. Yet I see figures in the clouds." Thistle spoke as if they were still lying in the clearing high above Bear Butte.

She took his hand and pulled him forward, and something fell away from his ankle.

"I can't," he said.

"Then trust your visions," Thistle insisted.

Fischer closed his eyes and focused, and in an instant the dizziness swept over him. He felt himself withdrawing from the desolate road and coming to rest in a place where all was peaceful. He saw the flickering glow of a candle, drew toward it with outstretched hands to cup around its flame. The light grew inside the protection of his hands, and he drew on its warmth. Then the face of a dragon appeared inside the flame. A silver cup. He would not open his eyes.

"I see a dragon," he said.

"Yes, good." Thistle nodded. "The dragon is what is underfoot, Belial. What else do you see?"

"A cup. And that's all." Fischer's eyes flew open. "What does it mean?"

"A challenge awaits," Thistle said. But Fischer hardly heard because at that moment he spotted a figure materializing from the rolling dust.

"Look," he said, pointing to what he first thought was a mirage. A hundred paces ahead a man sat in a white robe.

Thistle dropped Fischer's hand. "Solomon. Father!"

The snakes vanished, and the dust began to settle. Ahead the man rose to his feet, and shadows raced across the land like windswept clouds. A wave of relief washed over Fischer in a warm, electric flood. Was it possible? Solomon was there, just as Thistle had promised.

But then he noticed that something had changed. No crickets sang in the grass; no wind blew. Even the click of hail on the pavement had suddenly ended.

"Solomon!" Thistle called.

The man raised his head. Fischer stopped to allow Thistle to run forward, but as she left him, it took every bit of his strength not to call after her. The tall dark man smiled and held out his arms. Fischer knew he should be ecstatic, dancing for joy in fact, to see Thistle delivered safely to her father, but instead, as he watched her race toward Solomon with open arms, he felt only sadness. After all, what was he without her? Suddenly he was the old Fischer, his father's disappointment, the one who wasn't capable of winning anything.

No, don't, he told himself. The Keepers are together. Nothing else matters as much as that. But in his gloom he touched the Stone, and a little voice inside him objected: except that now you will lose her forever.

When Thistle had covered a few short feet of the distance that stretched between her and Solomon, Fischer heard music. He looked for a truck coming down the highway but saw only sheep grazing in the distance.

A movement caught his eye, something coming from over a rise in the pasture. Thistle stopped suddenly, and Solomon lowered his arms.

Fischer turned toward the strains of a circus tune, and all at once a clown with orange hair and white face paint appeared, walking briskly. Solomon ran toward Thistle, but Fischer could do nothing but gape as the clown drew nearer. His appearance evoked something painful and menacing, but Fischer could not put his finger on what it was, not even when the clown stopped and opened his white-gloved hands with a flourish.

"Ah, Belial," Thistle said, her voice barely audible, "I knew you would come."

"Miss me?" the clown asked.

Thistle spit in his direction.

"Such manners." Belial clucked his tongue. "A tiresome girl, although I guess I can scarcely call you a girl, now can I? And, Solomon, you're looking the worse for wear. But good news, your retirement is imminent."

Solomon's eyes blazed as he stepped forward.

Belial held up his hand. "The two of you are of little consequence now. Why, I'd have more trouble from new-born infants." He suddenly turned to face Fischer. "Or young men. Now, tell me, Fischer, how is it that you have saved me the trouble of bringing these two to their knees?"

Fischer's heart pounded with fear and anger. "It was an accident," he said, hating the sound of his voice. It was the tone he had once reserved for answering David's criticism.

"An accident?" The clown laughed. "I must know every detail."

"It was my mistake, not Thistle's," Fischer said. "So this is my problem."

"Ah, most certainly it is. But as I'm sure dear Thistle has told you, whodunit is not really my department."

"Then what is?" Fischer asked.

"Look closely, Fischer." Belial framed his face with his hands. "Do I remind you of someone?"

With a shudder, Fischer made the connection. "I remember you. You were there that day with my father at the circus, or was it in my dream—"

"No," Thistle cried out. "Leave him alone."

"Thistle." Belial waggled his finger. "You've had your moment. Don't you recall?"

Thistle met Fischer's gaze, but there was no comfort in her expression as Belial continued. Fischer slid his hands into his pockets and, at the touch of something smooth and warm, remembered the Stone.

"This moment is the boy's, as you're about to see. Fischer, forgive me. I'm afraid I must reveal your little secret."

Fischer held the Stone tightly.

"Yes," Belial said. "You do have a secret, don't you, Fischer? You have a play pretty. And I believe that once Thistle and Solomon know what it is, they will see that this business will have to be settled between the two of us." He made a beckoning gesture with his index finger. "Come now. Bring it out, so we can all see."

Fischer tried to resist but felt his hand leave his pocket.

His palm lifted and his fingers opened, revealing the Stone. He heard a cry behind him.

"Fischer." Thistle's voice was filled with anguish. "No."

When he turned, he saw that tears had sprung to her eyes.

"I don't blame you for desiring that Stone, my boy," Belial said. "It is a wondrous thing. It can make you strong and powerful, lion and leopard all in one. Your Thistle knows that. That's why she doesn't want you to have it."

Fischer's fingers folded over the Stone, and all at once power jolted him like a tidal wave and then washed through him. Thistle's eyes were fearful; the set of her mouth was perplexed. Didn't she trust him? If she did, why couldn't she see how much he needed the Stone?

"Fischer, put the Stone away," Thistle shouted.

"No," Belial said. "The boy is the Taker. He'll do with it as he pleases." He smiled at Fischer, and suddenly Fischer felt empowered, as though he had laid claim to something long denied him. Now the Stone could be his. He found himself returning Belial's smile.

"Fischer, the truth, do I look like a monster?" Belial held a hand over his heart.

"More trickery," Thistle shouted.

"But you have another little secret, don't you, stoic boy? You have grown affectionate of Thistle. You have feelings for her, deep feelings."

"What Fischer and I share is not your concern, Belial," Thistle said. "It cannot be altered, not even by you."

"It appears I've struck a nerve," Belial said. "Never fear, we shall explore that in due time. But first, Fischer, would you like to know what has become of the third of your little band, the one who dared stand in your way?" Belial's face collapsed into a tragic scowl. "He shattered your hopes, made you look a fool. He became an unbearable nuisance, didn't he?"

For a moment Fischer's heart seemed to skip, but then he rubbed the Stone in his hand. He was acutely aware of Thistle watching him and hoping his worried expression might hide the anticipation that had filled him. "What have you done?"

Belial placed his fingers to his lips, and suddenly a picture formed in Fischer's mind of a familiar figure in filthy shorts and T-shirt walking along the side of the highway. The figure hunched under his poncho as the rain beat harder against his back, shivering as another car slowed, then passed him by. It was David.

"Not such a brave boy now, is he?" Belial asked. "Not such a braaaave adventurer?"

"No, he's not," Fischer said, secretly pleased.

"You're right, my boy. David is a scoundrel, true enough, but he can sometimes appear worthy of admiration. He is bold and high-spirited and charming. I doubt it will surprise you to hear that these qualities have caught your own father's eye."

Fischer couldn't bear it. He grabbed up the Stone and held it high, feeling a whirl of emotions inside him. His father couldn't see him for what he was. He thought he was weak, defective. But what could he do? Grasping the Stone, he felt strong, as though nothing were out of the realm of possibility. Suddenly he realized that perhaps there was a way to change his father's heart.

"Fischer," Belial chided. "Oh, yes, you could use the Stone to win over dear old dad. But you must think, my boy. Because then you will no longer possess it."

Fischer felt the blood rush from his face.

"But there is something else you should consider. Something quite compelling. You could join me and keep the Stone yourself."

"No, I would never," Fischer said, turning to Thistle. But his words were weak and passionless, and his face grew hot with anger as he studied her grave expression. How could she question him?

"Ah, but you see, you've already considered it," Belial said. "And there is no shame in that, Fischer. You feel what the Stone offers when you hold it. It makes you believe that you are the strongest being on earth, as though you are invincible."

Before Fischer could answer, the clown figure suddenly transformed into the tall, elegant man from his dreams.

"You," Fischer whispered.

"May I make a confession?" Belial said. "I grapple with the idea that a man like your father is too blind, or uninterested, to see you as you truly are. A boy of great deeds and intelligence, a boy who has awakened from a deep sleep refreshed and willing to accept an unharnessed power. But I see your merit, Fischer. I have been watching you. I have chosen you to be the one. I have been waiting for a son for many, lonely years."

Fischer's mind swirled as he held fast to the Stone.

"Beware, Fischer," Thistle warned. "He will say anything to take the Stone for himself."

"Could I not say the same of you?" Belial shouted. "I know of the trickery you've used in trying to win this Stone. Was it truth to make the boy believe you cared for him?" Belial said. "When you want to gain the Taker's Stone with no thought of his own circumstance, but only to pay penance for what you did yourself."

What penance? Fischer felt stung as he whirled around to search Thistle's face. For as long as he could recall, his father had tricked him, holding his love out of his reach as though Fischer were a dog to tease. Had Thistle done the same? His hands became fists at his side.

"He lies," Thistle said. "Fischer, do not be lulled into believing that this is a game. There is much more at stake than that."

"Crafty Thistle. I can't let you avoid this opportunity to

bare your soul and make your confession. The jig is up, as they say. Tell Fischer why your mother befell her fate."

Tears streamed down Thistle's face as she turned to him. "I told you about that morning in 1811 when my father was called to the monastery and I accompanied him. But what I did not tell you is of more importance now. As a little girl I did not know the power of the Stones, but I saw my mother and my father guard them so earnestly, hide them away when I was near. Of course now I know they did so for my own good, but at the time I only knew that the Stones entranced me."

Fischer could not take his eyes away from Thistle. So she had felt drawn by the Stones as he had. Why had she never told him this?

"I wanted to hold them; they were so beautiful, perfect. I desired them for my own. So on that morning I went to the place where I had seen my mother hide the Stones and took one from her pouch." Thistle closed her eyes for a moment. "I confess, I grew bold as it glowed in my hand. My immediate thought was how courageous I was to have taken it, how clever I was to have accomplished the feat without my mother's knowledge. Then I heard my father calling my name, dropped the Stone into my apron pocket, and ran to go along with him on his business with the priests."

Fischer knew how Thistle's story would end. "And that's how Belial was able to have your mother killed while you and Solomon were away." He shuddered. "The Stones had been separated from the Keepers."

"It's true that I understand you much better than you might imagine, Fischer," Thistle said. "I know how difficult it is to hold the Stone and consider losing it. I know it only too well." Her gaze was full of love and sadness. "For before you, Fischer, I was the Taker."

*Now faith is the substance of things hoped
for, the evidence of things not seen.*

—Hebrews 11:1

CHAPTER TWENTY

Lightning flashed, and Belial's laughter rumbled out like the echo of thunder beyond the buttes. "A sweet tale. Truly poignant," he said. A stack of rock in the nearby pasture collapsed into a pile, and the sheep grazing in the fields raised their heads, chewing mechanically. "You'll forgive me if I fail to be moved. But after all, Thistle, this is water under the bridge."

Fischer felt joy, then pain. Which was real?

"Fischer, at my side not only will you possess the Stone, but I personally will see that you have everything, everything you have ever desired," Belial said. His body contorted like putty, then pulled and twisted into the shape of a young boy with turquoise-colored eyes. "This is one of my favorites," he said in a childlike voice. "But men prefer this one." The boy's body squeezed out and up like toothpaste from a tube until it molded into a woman's figure.

"You know me, don't you?" the woman asked. She lifted her hair over one shoulder and levitated an apple toward Fischer.

Belial smiled. "Fischer, you'll enjoy this," a familiar voice said. Where Eve had been moments earlier, now Thistle stood. She wore the long blue dress that he remembered so well, and her pale hair fell over her shoulders. Fischer's heart lifted, and he rose to his feet, but then he saw that this Thistle's blue eyes were void of light.

"Deceiver!"

Fischer turned. The real Thistle stood behind him.

"Ah, Fischer, look at me," the Thistle image said. "Am I not everything you have ever wanted? What more could you desire?"

Again the figure transformed, grew into the shape of a man, tall like Fischer, but older, sandy-haired, gray at the sideburns, with wire-rimmed glasses over gray eyes. Fischer felt a stab of pain as he recognized his father. "Fischer, I want so much to be proud of you. Can't you see that I do? And now you have the chance to prove to me that you want that, too." His father held out his hands, and his gaze fell on Fischer. "Give me the Stone, son."

Fischer felt a hand touch his shoulder, Thistle's hand. "Fischer, wake up and remember who you are!"

And who was that? Fischer wanted to ask. But suddenly he remembered Thistle's words earlier in the day: that the

Stones played with men's hearts. He dropped the Stone into his pocket, and the power instantly drained from his body, leaving him weak and sickened. Somehow he refused to do what his mind was screaming out to do, snatch the Stone back up again.

"Trust your visions," Thistle whispered.

Fischer suddenly knew what she meant. He had been so engrossed in what he thought he had to have—the Stone, his father, Thistle—that he had forgotten to trust what he couldn't see. What he couldn't see was the world that ran like a hidden current inside the one he lived in, the one that raced, obscured, just under the surface of the present. He closed his eyes, and the dizziness began. He touched the Stone, and the light grew inside his head, enormous and encompassing as daybreak.

Fischer saw the moving shapes and shadows. He did not know what they were, but they reminded him of the branches that held the prayer cloths, the figures that lit within the stained glass windows of Grandpa's church. "The eye can see only as far as the horizon." It was Grandpa's words that he suddenly remembered. "But that doesn't mean that it ends there, pal."

"This girl doesn't want what's best for you. She's holding you back from what you could be, son."

Fischer opened his eyes. He saw his father, standing in front of him, his brow furrowed.

"Don't let her come between us. Give me the Stone."
His father's expression was wary. There was something un-
natural about the flatness of his eyes.

At that moment the wind began to race by Fischer's
legs, lifting his shirttail behind him like a cape, whipping
his hair against his face and making it difficult to see as
sand stung him. He reached into his pocket and pulled out
the Stone and staggered back as the rush of its power entered him with all the urgency of a roar.

"I knew you would come to your senses." Now Belial
stood in his father's place.

"Yes," Fischer said. "I have."

Belial's eyes were suddenly as red as the last smoldering
light of day. Fischer felt an overpowering sense of release
and then a vast mindlessness that seemed like peace.

He extended his hand, with the Stone in his palm.
"Take it," he said.

"Fischer, no!" Thistle cried.

In a single motion Fischer tossed the Stone high into
the air. He saw the light of the Stone in Thistle's eyes as
she reached out for it. As Fischer had guessed, Belial
lunged toward the Stone, toward Thistle, and instantly, he
stepped between them. Belial hesitated—only for a second, but it was enough. Fischer stared him dead in the eye.
"I know you," he whispered.

Then Belial's face contorted, and the skies overhead

seemed to open as though they had cracked. As Thistle reached out, caught the Stone, and held it in her fist, Fischer felt an immense emptiness that left him too weak to stand. Then he was on his knees, dreaming he saw Thistle standing. He tried to blink and focus, but the urge to close his eyes grew far too great, and he allowed himself to collapse into the deep and soothing lake of unconsciousness.

When Fischer's eyes blinked open, he saw the repetitive flash of lights overhead. At first he thought he must be in the truck on the highway headed for Castle Rock, but then he made out billboards, buildings, and the glow of streetlights.

"Fischer, you're awake."

Suddenly Thistle's face appeared. He sat up, though his head was pounding, then lowered himself back onto the soft seat. He saw chrome buttons, the glass square of windows.

"Where are we?" he asked.

"Don't worry. We are safe." Thistle reached out and touched his forehead. "You've been unconscious for some time now."

Then Fischer remembered. Castle Rock. Belial. "What happened?"

"The Taker's Stone has been returned."

Fischer was too tired to ask more. He only wanted to be there, with Thistle. But then he saw the tears in her eyes.

He struggled and this time succeeded in sitting up. "You're leaving, aren't you?"

"No," she said. "You are leaving, Fischer. You must join David at the airport and go home. Belial is gone for a time, but he will not stay away. Solomon insists that we take our leave quickly. As you know, the Keepers must stay together."

Fischer nodded. "Right. Of course. But where is Solomon?"

Thistle cast a sidelong glance at their driver. "Solomon found one of the cars abandoned at the roadside to be open and was able to . . . borrow it." She raised her eyebrows. "He has become quite the mechanical genius after all our years of travel."

Solomon's face appeared in the rearview mirror. "Tools of the trade, I fear. How is our young warrior?"

"Not bad, considering," Fischer said, though the pain he felt knowing that he was about to leave Thistle was far greater than any he had suffered so far.

Solomon laughed. "Well said. There are only a few miles left until we reach our destination. You'll forgive me if I don't add much to the conversation. It's been quite some time since I have driven a vehicle. I must proceed with caution." He met Fischer's eye in the mirror, and Fischer smiled back appreciatively.

"What will happen to you now?" he asked Thistle as she climbed into the backseat and sat beside him.

"We will wander." She shrugged. "As we did when you and David found our fire."

"But is this it? Will I ever see you again?"

"I believe that we will see each other again, yes. But until that time I want you to remember my words. What we share cannot be altered. Our bond is sacred."

Fischer was unable to speak. He took Thistle's hand and held it tight.

"I told you that these events flow from a source, a wellspring. One day I will know why they have occurred."

Fischer studied her. "Will I ever know?"

"You will," she said. "I swear it."

"It is time, Thistle," Solomon said. He smiled at Fischer. "As I have heard it said, we are there."

Fischer looked out the window and recognized the Pierre airport. He wanted only to be with Thistle a few moments more.

"Farewell then." Solomon grasped Fischer's hand.

"Good-bye," Fischer said. Turning to Thistle, he whispered, "No matter how long, no matter what, I'll know you," he said. He kissed her quickly, then, raw with anguish, pushed open the door and slid out into the night.

Through the glass doors of the building, he spotted David, pacing near the security check. He turned back to tell Thistle that he had found David, to turn and see her face once more, but when he did, he found nothing where the car had been but an empty curb, and beyond, a sky full of shimmering stars.

/ / /

WSTR

Leeland, Georgia

Sunday, September 9

This is one beautiful day here in the South. Clear skies expected through the weekend, slightly cooler than usual with highs of seventy-five and lows of sixty-three. Now tell me seriously, folks, isn't this one of those days that just make you happy to be alive?

/ / /

To him that overcometh will I give to eat of the hidden manna, and will give him a white stone, and in the stone a new name written, which no man knoweth saving he that receiveth it. —Revelation 2:17

CHAPTER TWENTY-ONE

In the stillness of the old stone church, Fischer sat holding his newly christened baby brother, Thomas. He stared up at the stained glass above the crucifix until he heard approaching footsteps. His mother and father walked toward him, leaving his aunt Kathy, uncle Matthew, and David to make conversation with the priest.

"Ready to go?" his mother asked. She gently lifted Thomas from Fischer's arms. "I think Thomas is ready for a nap."

"Mom." Fischer kept his eyes glued to the floor. "Do you mind if I don't come with you?"

His mother stopped fussing with the baby blanket she pulled from the bag on her shoulder. "Why?"

"I just want to sit here awhile. Only a few minutes," he told her.

Fischer's mother studied him. "Sure you're all right?"

She placed a hand on his head the way she used to when he was a child.

"Perfect," Fischer said. "Really. It was a crazy summer, and now with school and all, I just want a minute to think."

"You stay as long as you want. I worry about you, kiddo. Seems you've been different, quieter since you came home from White Horse."

"Must be that dreaded adolescence you keep talking about." Fischer smiled.

"You've never been adolescent, Fischer." His mother laughed. "You were born a hundred years old."

A chill ran through Fischer.

"Father Florio is coming for lunch," his mother continued. "You know how he loves cucumber and dill sandwiches. And I've asked some of the neighbors in."

"I'll be there, I promise. I'll be home before Father Florio's into his second glass of iced tea," Fischer said.

Fischer's father appeared and placed a hand on her shoulder.

Fischer's mother tucked a corner of Thomas's blanket under his tiny feet. "All set," she said. "Fischer is going to stay a little longer."

"Oh?" Fischer's father cast him a curious glance, then smiled at his wife and new baby. "I'll meet you at the car. I want a word alone with Fischer."

A sudden sense of dread grew inside Fischer as he watched his mother walk away from them.

"David's been telling me that football tryouts are coming up soon," his father said. "I thought you and I could get in some practice after lunch."

Fischer raised his eyes to meet his father's. "I'm not trying out for football this year. Gund at the museum—he's offered me a job after school, and I'm going to take it."

"You are?" His father studied him. "So you're willing to give up your chance on the team?"

"I'm not good enough to make the team, Dad. And the truth is, I don't want to."

"I can't say I'm not disappointed." His father hesitated. "And I'd argue with you, but you seem to know what you want."

Fischer looked up, surprised.

David suddenly appeared from behind. "Yeah, Fischer's finally found nirvana in that mausoleum of a museum. Personally I can't imagine a more boring way to pass the time than having a job in that dustbin, but hey, different strokes."

"After this summer I didn't think you'd mind boring," Fischer said.

David's smug smile disappeared, and Fischer's father looked at both boys curiously.

"Well, I give you credit for taking on a job," he said.

Fischer nodded. "Thanks." Something new was in his father's expression as he met his eye again.

"Look, I'm out of here." David began to back away, dropping his sunglasses into place from the top of his head. "Food awaits. Let's jet."

His father took out his car keys. "Sure I can't change your mind?"

Fischer nodded and smiled. "You go on. I'll only be a little while longer."

Finally the door closed, leaving Fischer alone. He felt his shoulders relax against the wooden pew.

Born a hundred. Well, he felt that way. Though he had been home for only six weeks, they had been the longest six weeks of his life. The morning after he and David had flown back, he had woken up in his room at David's to find nothing changed. Except that instead of finding Thistle waiting for him in the corner chair, now there was only his jacket draped over the arm. When he dug into its front pocket, it was empty.

David had also woken that day, seemingly his same old self. If he remembered Thistle or what had happened in South Dakota, he never mentioned it.

Fischer had thought that was okay, for the best some-how, but he was glad when his mother called to say that he had a new baby brother and Uncle Matt and Aunt Kathy had driven him home to Leeland.

Then suddenly his father was there, and both of his parents were preoccupied with the baby. He tried being cheerful, tried to be his old self, but the truth was, he wasn't. He didn't sleep well at night, preferring to stay up late reading. When he was out during the day, he watched people's eyes in a way he never had before, and when he walked beside the river, he searched the shadows near the rocks and the dark places where the trees overhung the water as though something might be hiding inside them.

Fischer took one last glance at the crucifix and stood. He should get home. This was Thomas's big day, and he didn't want his mother worrying about him. He scooted to the end of the pew, turned into the aisle, and found himself staring up at the stained glass panels set in the walls.

Each panel depicted a scene from the parables, and the one he looked at was of a woman. "The Woman and the Lost Silver Coin," a mosaic marker read below. The woman seemed more like a girl to Fischer, pale-skinned with long corn silk hair and eyes as blue as hyacinth. She was shown stooping, one hand on the table, the other on some object on the rough floor beneath. The lost silver coin. But was there some kind of writing etched into it? Fischer squinted hard. Not writing, but the features of a man's face. He leaned back for a moment and frowned. A man's face that looked very much like Solomon's. Fischer bent toward the glass. But as he did, the face on the coin suddenly dissolved, and another took its place. He was staring at his own image. Fischer stepped back, holding on to the back of a pew for support.

When he whirled around to face the wall again, the coin's face was empty, and the woman in the panel bore no resemblance to Thistle at all.

The eye can see only as far as the horizon. Fischer recalled Grandpa's words. But the world beyond it is unending.

Fischer turned and made his way down the aisle, his heart pounding at the notion of what he had seen in the stained glass panel. He pushed open the doors of the church and stood on the stone steps, absorbing the brilliant sunshine. It was the comfort of it that made him think of other days, days without warmth or light. But it also made him think of now, this life, with his mother and Thomas and, in some new way, even his father.

Fischer walked down the steps, then hesitated. Was it truly the sunlight, or what he had seen back in the church that warmed him? It didn't matter. He had seen and might see again, so some sadness rose out of him and scattered like ash. Passersby on the sidewalk moved around him like currents. Suddenly, aware of where he was, Fischer stepped into the flow. Without a backward glance, he matched the stride of the strangers on his left and his right, feeling an unexplainable happiness overtake him as he began the long walk home.

Juv.
PZ
7
.R91536
Tak
1999

Lebanon Valley College
Bishop Library
Annville, PA 17003

GAYLORD RG